VOLT II

Mark
Hope you enjoy
the Book!

Doug Chatman

VOLT II

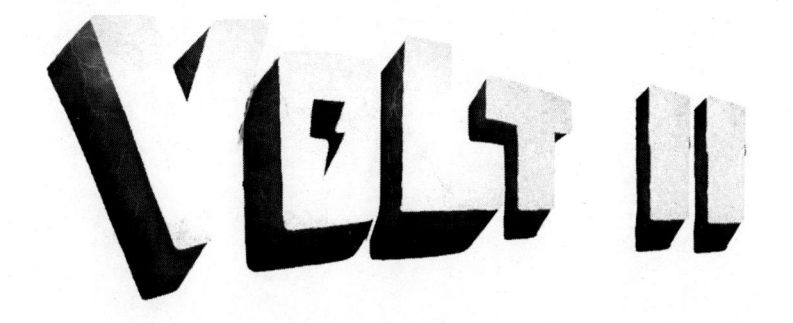

THE MONSTER WITHIN

VIGILANTE OF
LORD'S TREASURES | **DOUG CHATMAN**

TATE PUBLISHING
AND ENTERPRISES, LLC

Volt II
Copyright © 2015 by Doug Chatman. All rights reserved.

No part of this publication may be reproduced, stored in a retrieval system or transmitted in any way by any means, electronic, mechanical, photocopy, recording or otherwise without the prior permission of the author except as provided by USA copyright law.

This novel is a work of fiction. Names, descriptions, entities, and incidents included in the story are products of the author's imagination. Any resemblance to actual persons, events, and entities is entirely coincidental.

The opinions expressed by the author are not necessarily those of Tate Publishing, LLC.

Published by Tate Publishing & Enterprises, LLC
127 E. Trade Center Terrace | Mustang, Oklahoma 73064 USA
1.888.361.9473 | www.tatepublishing.com

Tate Publishing is committed to excellence in the publishing industry. The company reflects the philosophy established by the founders, based on Psalm 68:11,
"The Lord gave the word and great was the company of those who published it."

Book design copyright © 2015 by Tate Publishing, LLC. All rights reserved.
Cover design by Junriel Boquecosa
Interior design by Honeylette Pino

Published in the United States of America

ISBN: 978-1-63418-876-0
1. Fiction / Science Fiction / General
2. Fiction / Fantasy / General
15.02.16

CHAPTER 1

The stadium lights illuminate the London night sky. Everyone in the sold-out arena holds their breath as Hank "The Tank" Jamerson positions himself for the penalty kick and the potential win and championship. The blonde-haired giant, wearing a navy jersey with a wide horizontal gold stripe stretching over his pecks, stops the steady stream of sweat running down his face with his forearm. Shaking it off his arm, he digs in his right foot in takeoff position as he eyes the opposing goalie. A small, cocky smirk appears on his face, as if reliving the previous foul that landed him in the precarious spot. Hank had attempted to score with a header that would have given the Gold Knights a point over France's Red Dragons with just seconds left to play. But instead, a French defender managed to trip "The Tank" just as he was about to leap in position, bringing about the penalty kick.

The referee blows his whistle for the game to proceed. Stretching confidently, Hank takes a deep breath and takes three monstrous steps and lays into the soccer ball with all his might. The ball lifts off the ground, hooking back to the left as the Red Dragon goalie leaps up in an attempt to block the kick. The ball sails just past the goalie with him only getting his fingertips on the ball.

The ball wraps up in the net along with the thunderous ovation of the entire stadium.

The Gold Knights charge Jamerson as he kneels with both arms raised in the air in front of him. The crowd chants, "Tank, Tank, Tank!" with Hank thrusting his arms up and down in unison with the chants as if his arms are cannons. The team jumps and dog piles their hero.

Pastor Phillips slaps his hands together and jumps in the air in his living room in reaction to the Gold Knight's victory.

"Yes!" he shouts at the television.

"How about that man!" Phillips said as he slaps a shocked Dustin on the shoulder as he sat on the sofa.

Dustin sits with a blank stare at the TV.

"Yeah, how about that," Dustin replies in a flat monotone.

Widening and then rolling his eyes, Dustin couldn't believe what he just witnessed. Clearly, he doesn't share the same enthusiasm as the pastor.

"Oh, yeah," the pastor replies.

Pastor Phillips stands frozen for a moment with his fists up in a celebratory manner. He slowly lowers his arms, realizing that his enjoyment might be causing his guest some discomfort.

A bit of guilt comes over Dustin as he realizes he is keeping the pastor from celebrating the way he wants to in his own home. He tries his best to lighten the mood by putting on a smirking grin.

"Don't get me wrong, sir. I just don't know why it had to be him to score the win for the championship."

"Well, at least be happy for the rest of the team," the pastor requests.

"I am. Just, why him?" Dustin said with a defeated smile.

The pastor seemingly could see Dustin reliving an unpleasant past in his mind.

"I know, you just have to let that pain go," the pastor said. "Come on, still peckish? We have tons of food left!"

"Oh, I'm stuffed," Dustin says as he rubs his gut. "But I need to tell Lucy thanks for the snacks."

Dustin pulls himself up from the couch and walks through the kitchen to thank the pastor's wife, Lucy, for the treats during the championship game. He says good-bye to Sharon, the church secretary, who was invited to watch the game too, but spent most of the evening visiting with the pastor's wife in the kitchen. Then he thanks the pastor for having him over.

Dustin bends down and picks up his black backpack and flings it over his shoulder. The pastor's eyebrows rise as he seemingly realized what is in the backpack.

"You always have it with you?" the pastor asks as he nods his head, acknowledging his weathered pack.

"Well, you never know when duty may call," he replies with raised eyebrows.

Dustin glances down at his watch.

"It's getting late, so I better be off," Dustin said. "I'll see you tomorrow."

"Okay, sounds good," the pastor replies, giving Dustin a hearty pat on the back, while he focuses his eyes on Dustin's backpack as he steps out.

Dustin heads down the sidewalk back to his home at Berthel Church. As he walks home, he can hear the occasional celebration going on in various establishments and residences.

During the jubilation, he would enviably hear the chant, "Tank, Tank, Tank!"

Letting out a deflated sigh, he rolls his eyes. Dustin ponders his strong dislike for Hank Jamerson. In his mind, he knows it is wrong to harbor such bad feelings for "the Tank." He thought that maybe the ill feelings would start to dissipate over time, but Hank's recent stardom brought all those sore feelings back to the surface. It had been a little over five years since he became acquaintaned with Hank, five years of trying to recover.

"Of all people, why Hank?" Dustin utters to himself as he continues his way home. He's unsure if he is asking God why he allowed Hank's success or if he was just trying to come to grips himself with his adversary's accomplishments.

As Dustin walks through the dimly lit business district, he suddenly hears what seems to be a group of men yelling loudly at each other. His estimation had them a block over from his current location. Curiosity got the best of him as he investigates the noise. He locates the ruckus, and finds a group of twelve men outside a sports pub. They appear to be broken into two groups, eight versus four. The four are wearing red in support of their French team, which seems to rub fans of the Gold Knights the wrong way. The argument quickly turns into a brawl as the four French men find themselves in obvious trouble as the Knights' supporters quickly have an upper hand on the situation.

One man in a navy blue pullover grabs a man in red and swings him onto the hood of a car parked in the street. The man winces in pain as his attacker grabs and pulls him off the hood. The attacker went back to swing when the French man asks a question that catches the bully off guard.

"Don't tell me he's with you?" the man asks in his heavy French accent.

His assailant turns around only to find the creature, VoLt, standing in front of him. He's unable get a word out before VoLt grabs him by his shirt and flings him over his shoulder where he strategically lands on two other attackers. Three down, five to go. VoLt leaps in the air and tackles two others as they continue to pound on the foreign fans. The men dressed in blue grunt in pain as the creature lands on both of them. Popping to his feet, VoLt stands up and stares at the last three. By now, they are retreating and running off in different directions.

VoLt surveys the five drunks as they lay in two different piles on the sidewalk. The four French men stand together, amazed at the creature before them. One wipes his bloody nose while another tends to a cut on his brow. All four were winded and anxious to see VoLt's next move.

"My apologizes for their poor hospitality," VoLt says as he slightly bows.

Before they could respond, he quickly scales the building by using the gutters and window edges only to disappear over the rooftop. As VoLt escapes, he asks himself why he didn't bother to cleanse those eight assailants, but he realizes that sometimes you can't cleanse the drunk and stupid.

VoLt leaps over one alley onto another rooftop, and then another. He had to admit to himself, he enjoyed testing out his abilities and his agility when the opportunity presented itself. Especially at night, after answering "a call" and the duty was done, he could push himself in order to find his limits. And the fact that he has some built-in frustration only fuels his desire to push himself.

He feels himself pick up speed across the rooftops as flashes of Hank enter in his mind. Letting out a low growl, he leaps over the quick approaching alley and easily sails through the air only to land with the same ease. He even surprised himself with that little test.

"Okay, better quit while I'm ahead."

VoLt makes his way down the side of a building and lands behind a row of tall hedges. He takes off the cloak and medallion and then slides off the backpack that he wears under the cloak. Dustin pulls his shirt and shoes from the backpack that he had recently began to tote around with him whenever he went out. As he shoves the cloak in the backpack, he glances down at the gold V-shaped medallion as it faintly glows, lying on the ground. His mind flashes back nearly two years ago to the moment when he first saw the glowing V-shaped metal as it hung around the neck of VoLt where Tim Warner once stood just mere moments before.

Prior to that, at Tim's request, they took a walk through the woods of the Warner Farm. Dustin recalled how he felt obligated to accompany him as he continued to ramble on about certain events that occurred during the early stages of World War II.

Tim had told an extraordinary story of how he was injected with a special serum by a demented professor named Lucas Zen after an attempt to save his best friend's life. In a freak incident in Zen's laboratory, a gorilla broke loose and attacked Zen. The professor shot the creature at the exact same moment when an act of God allowed lightning to strike the beast. In that instant, an alteration of the element configuration occurred to the special serum and the gold bullets that struck the gorilla.

Only after the injection of the altered serum, Professor Zen placed the three bloodstained gold bullets into Tim's hand in a hateful sarcastic gesture. Little did Zen know what the immediate reaction would be once Tim came in contact with the three gold bullets. Tim began to transform into a hideous powerful beast that had the ability to overcome adversaries as well as the ability to help others break the grip that their controlling sin had over their lives.

Being able to escape with his newfound powers, he found refuge at Jessica Parsons. After being told of the experimentation, Jessica felt the urge to take the three bullets and have them molded into a shape that would stand for the new alter ego of Tim Warner and the calling from God to serve as VoLt, the Vigilante of Lord's treasures.

Cautiously picking up the gold medallion and placing it in his backpack, he relives the moment when Tim, in the form of VoLt, chased him down in that dark forest and injected him with the same mysterious formula that ran through Tim. A cold shiver runs up and down Dustin's spine as the tries to shake the haunting memory. Peering from behind the hedge, he's able to see that the coast is clear. Dustin emerges from the bushes and dusts off the twigs that cling to his clothes. Taking a deep breath, he makes track back home.

The celebration began to subside as the cool night wore on. Now, all that was left were the nonstop sports reports on the television and the front covers of every newspaper that quickly began to pop up on the corner newspaper stands with Hank "the Tank" Jamerson splattered all over them.

"Why Hank?" Dustin again asks as he kicks a lonely pebble on the sidewalk. The rock skids and bounces across the concrete. He watches it land in a street gutter, where he stops for a moment to hear the pebble rattle its way into the sewer system below.

"Score."

Dustin raises his arms in a celebrative moment only to quickly bring them down. Glancing around in embarrassment, he hopes no one saw that moment of immaturity.

CHAPTER 2

A young woman, donning shades and wearing a long navy blue coat, enters the lobby of the Sheraton Hotel, with her vibrant red hair cascading down onto her shoulders. The lobby is filled with news reporters from the BBC and various London newspapers, and for a moment, she unwillingly catches the eye of each reporter at some point during the stride across the lobby. One particular BBC sports reporter recognizes the redhead immediately as she tries to hide behind her big, black sunglasses. He jumps to his feet and hops over the cable cords that are sprawled out all over the lobby to catch her.

"Ginger! Hey, Ginger! Come on! Help me with this exclusive!" the reporter yells.

The woman turns around sharply to shoot a glare at the obnoxious man that even he is able see through the dark shades. She continues walking past the elevators down the hallway, while he pursues. All the other reporters watch and glance back at each other as if they feared they just missed out on the scoop of the day.

"Come on, Ginger," he said as he lowered his voice as he closes in on her.

By now, they were clear of the lobby and far enough down the hallway where the secrecy was gone.

"Gin, Come on! Please! Scratch my back and I'll scratch yours."

"Gil!" she said, abruptly turning around and stopping dead in her tracks. "What do you want?"

"You know what I want. I want the first exclusive interview with the star. Hank "the Tank" Jamerson!" Gil said as he fanned his hands above him, giving Hank the star treatment.

"He's still sleeping."

Gil is already smoothing out his shirt and tie and running his fingers through his hair, indicating he was going to get his way. He glances down at her hand holding a tall cup of coffee.

"Is that coffee for him?"

"Ugh!"

"That means he'll be up soon," he nags.

"Okay, Gil, what's in it for me?" she asks, annoyed.

Gil's expression quickly transitions from desperation to enjoyment.

"Well, you know, I might be able to help you get assigned to a big story if you like."

She slightly rolls her eyes as she contemplates helping out the BBC's number one sports reporter. A recent journalism major graduate herself, Ginger had yet to land the big story to get her noticed. Ginger had been a random field reporter for BBC3. Her only clout seemed to be being the girlfriend of Hank "the Tank" Jamerson. The Tank's Tink, as she'd been called around the television station and in a few newspapers.

VoLt II

"Rumor has it, they still need a break on the whole VoLt thing," Gil said. "Maybe I can convince the big guy that you're the one with the spunk to scoop it."

She looks at him with skepticism. Pausing for a moment, she slightly rolls her eyes and then looks sternly at Gil.

"Okay, Okay. But if you don't come through, I'll have Tank rip your bloody arms off."

"Deal!" Gil said as he snaps his fingers to get his cameraman's attention, who had kept his distance, ready to pounce at his master's demand.

Ginger uses a waving hand gesture to Gil, instructing him to step back, which he ignores as he looks back behind him to make sure his cameraman was on the move. She knocks lightly on the door of the hotel room.

"Hank, honey, it's me," she said to the door. "Hank, you awake?"

Rustling can be heard on the other side of the door. She bites her lip as she waits for a response from the sleeping giant.

"Did you get my coffee?" the muffled voice asks behind the door.

"Yep," Ginger answers as she motions to Gil to back down a bit more. She knew not to agitate Hank so early in the morning.

The door opens and Hank stands there in nothing but his boxer shorts.

"Hank, put some clothes on," she said as she hands him the coffee.

She gingerly pushes him back into the room, making sure that the cameraman isn't able to get film of the six foot three muscle freak in his briefs. She quickly turns around and holds up one finger to Gil, indicating she needs a moment with Hank. The eagerness on Gil's face indicates he is on the verge of exploding with excitement. Ginger calmly turns around, steps in the room, and closes the door behind her.

Hank slowly sips his coffee as Ginger searches around the room for some decent clothes for Hank to wear for his exclusive interview. She approaches the subject cautiously.

"Hank, honey? Gil from the BBC would like to have the first interview with you."

Ginger runs her fingers through his bleached blonde bed head hair. Trying to pull it off as a loving gesture, but more importantly, trying to make him look presentable. Hank rolls his eyes and rolls his head as if fighting off a headache. He brushes her hand aside.

"Now?" he asks.

"I know it's early, but if you give him the exclusive, then he said he'd help me get a big story at work."

"Sounds like he might want more than that."

"Thanks, Hank. Please, a little respect."

"What's he going to pay me?"

"Pay you?"

"Yeah, I got everyone wanting to speak to me. And some are willing to pay big money to do it. Why should he be any different?"

"Please, Hank, can you do this for me?"

Hank pauses for a moment. He takes another drink of his coffee and shakes his head side to side, as if trying to pop his neck.

"Uh, sorry, babe, but no."

"Uhh! Why, Hank?"

"If he wants to be the first, then he's gotta pay up."

Hank turns around sipping his coffee, limping back toward his bed.

"Are you hurt?" she asks in an annoyed tone.

"Ehhh, no," he mumbles as he sets the coffee down on the nightstand and flops into bed.

"Well, I am," she says quietly to herself. "Thanks, Hank."

Turning around, she takes a deep breath as she opens the door, preparing herself to break the news to Gil that he wouldn't be getting the exclusive just yet.

Moments later, Ginger is trying to calm an agitated Gil.

"What do you mean I would have to pay up?" Gil asks, his hands on his hips, almost pouting for not getting his way.

"Sorry, Gil. He's not much for charity today," Ginger responds, still stinging from Hank's most recent selfishness.

Gil looks at Ginger as she has difficulty looking at him in the face. A small smile creeps in on his face.

"Well, hey, if I get the payment, can I have the exclusive?"

Ginger's eyes widened as she looks up at Gil.

"Yes! I'll make sure of it!"

She grabs Gil and gives him a huge hug, catching him off guard.

"Heh-hey. It's okay. Thanks, Ginger. I'll make sure the chief knows what you did for us."

"Thank you, Gil! Thank you so much!"

A sparkle returns to her eyes.

"I'll let Hank know," she says as she turns around, only to come to a brief stop. "But maybe I'll let him sleep in a bit before I let him know." She turns back to Gil.

"Yeah, maybe that's best," Gil says in response with a tone that somehow insinuates that the sports star might be losing a bit of his luster in Gil's eyes.

CHAPTER 3

A silver Mercedes pulls up in front of a shimmering, ten-story building. The structure, consisting mostly of mirrored glass, stands proudly amongst the other new construction of buildings in the new business district. The driver of the car, dressed in black, steps out and opens the back door, allowing Mr. Gustav to climb out.

Mr. Gustav looks around at the renovation taking place in the business district. The bright, shimmering new buildings are a far cry from the rubble of the old business district that he saw on his last business trip to London. He and two of his business associates narrowly escaped with their lives as Zen's fusion regenerator all but leveled the area.

Standing there, he quickly straightens out his gray business coat and nods to the driver as if telling him that he'll be back in a moment. The driver looks around and gets back into the car as Mr. Gustav proceeds to the lobby of the London Science Research Company, the LSRC as the media has been referring it.

Gustav walks into the lobby and approaches the reception desk where a member of the building's security guard is stationed.

"Yes, can I help you?" the guard asks.

"Yes, sir. I have a meeting with Dr. Irvine," Gustav says. "The last name is Gustav."

The security guard checks a list on a clipboard and then checks the computer screen in front of him.

"I'm sorry, but I don't have your name on the list," the guard says flatly.

"Are you kidding me? I've traveled all this way on his request and he didn't even bother to have me put on the list?" Gustav says in an annoyed tone.

The guard looks at Gustav skeptically as if he has been trained to assume everyone is guilty and very few are innocent. He reaches over, picks up the telephone, and dials a four-digit extension. There are a couple of rings, then a female voice answers the phone.

"Dr. Irvine's office. This is Sylvia. Can I help you?" the receptionist answers.

"Yes, Sylvia. This is Phil in the lobby. I have a Mr. Gustav down here. He indicates that he has an appointment with Dr. Irvine."

There is a noticeable pause, then a sudden frazzled Sylvia replies.

"Uh, okay. Yes. Send him right up please."

"Okay. Thank you." the guard answers in an even more skeptical tone.

He hangs up the phone and stares at Mr. Gustav with a look that indicates he doesn't quite agree with Sylvia.

"Office 10-G. Take the lift to the tenth floor. His office is on your right at the end."

"Thank you." Mr. Gustav replies with a confident tone as he makes his way to the elevator.

"What do you mean, he's here?" Dr. Irvine asks Sylvia nervously, looking around for his appointment book. The fifty-something-year-old physician feels the pockets of his white lab coat, hoping to find some kind of note that would remind him of the visit. "Is he supposed to be coming here today?"

The doctor nervously wipes his bald head while frantically smoothing out his remaining hairs on both sides.

"I don't have anything indicating that," she answers in a panicked tone as she quickly straightens up some of the loose papers scattered throughout the lab.

Then they hear the door open to the receptionist area as they both freeze. The doctor motions to Sylvia to go to her desk to formally greet him. She runs her hands over her dark blonde hair to smooth it out and then straightens her black business dress. Just as Sylvia reaches the door, it abruptly opens, nearly catching her in the nose.

In walks a short, bearded, Middle Eastern man with jet black hair and dark brown skin. He walks with confidence in his tan Italian suit as he surveys the cluttered, yet highly technical laboratory. Knowing he nearly hit Sylvia with the door, he does not bother to acknowledge her.

"How are we doing, Doctor?" Gustav asks, looking around the laboratory.

"Uh, well. We are making progress, but we—"

"Progress? Not completion?" Gustav asks with a disappointed glare, interrupting Irvine before he could finish.

"I'm trying my best. I don't know where this research started initially, Mr. Gustav, but it's very complex and somewhat unethical."

"We are not paying you to judge whether our research is ethical or not! We are paying you to enhance and finish the invention!" Gustav barks.

The doctor stands still with a look of an internal battle going on, the battle between his bank account and his conscience. The money appears to have won this battle.

"You're right, you're right. My apologies, but you will aid me if the authorities happen to catch wind of what I'm doing here? I mean, after all, we are right under their nose," the doctor said, looking up, as if he's constantly being watched.

"That's exactly why we came to you. They wouldn't think to look in one of their own buildings for a project like this," Gustav proudly states.

Gustav seems to take in some delight at causing Dr. Irvine so much stress.

"So, what about the progress?" Gustav asks.

The doctor sits down at his lab stool and spins around to the notes on the table.

"Well, I found a way to enhance the serum that would substantially enhance the current effect. Almost creating a turbo or GT version of the kronog," the doctor explains, "but the individual would need to be in tip top shape. A thoroughbred, so to speak."

Gustav stood beside Irvine, rubbing his beard with his right hand while the left held his right elbow.

"I see. So we just need to find the right specimen."

Gustav looks over and catches a glimpse of the front page of the *London Times* that lies on the end of the lab table. A picture of Tank Jamerson covers the front page.

Raising an eyebrow, he says, "I think I might know the perfect specimen."

Gustav reaches over and picks up the newspaper. Holding it in front of him, an evil grin appears under his beard.

CHAPTER 4

The church bell chimes twelve times. Dustin rubs his stomach.

"Finally! I'm starving," he says as he reaches around to make sure his wallet is indeed in his back pocket.

He grabs his brown leather jacket and makes his way from his basement office to the front doors. As he comes up the stairway to the foyer, he hears the church secretary speaking to someone.

"He should be around here somewhere," Sharon says.

Casually, Dustin proceeds up the stairway. Whether they were talking about him or the head pastor didn't concern him in the least.

"I'm sorry, what was your name again?" Sharon asks.

"Ginger."

Dustin stops dead in his tracks. Panic rushes through his body. Should he hide or should he run up to greet her? He moves slightly in position to where he could see her. Ginger has her back turned to him. He recognizes her shape and her red hair. Suddenly he feels the pain from the last time he saw her. Emotions run wild inside of him. With all the mental strength he has, he climbs up the next step, then the next, each step feeling like his feet were treading in thick, wet concrete. He reaches the top step and forces a smile.

"Ginger?" he asks.

Both Ginger and Sharon turn toward Dustin.

"There he is!" Sharon says as she raises her arms in his direction.

"Dustin!" Ginger says as she runs over to greet him with a hug.

"What are you doing here?" he asks, cautiously returning the embrace.

"Your mom told me where you were."

Dustin pulls back from the hug.

"Oh, mmm. Mom told you?" Dustin asks as he makes a mental note to contact his mother.

"Yeah! You know, you really need to call her more."

"Oh, I will."

"Wow, look at you!" she says, looking over his black shirt and gray slack outfit. "You're doing it!"

"Uh, yeah, I guess so," Dustin replies.

"This is so your calling," she states. "You set out to do this and you're doing it!"

"Thanks."

His actual calling caused him to briefly widen his eyes as he tries to match her excitement.

"And you! You look great!" he says. She looked so good to him, it hurt. "I was just on my way to lunch. Care to join me?" he asks.

"Love to!"

His heart races, but for so many reasons.

They walked over to the deli down the street from the church. They grab their sandwiches and sit at the pub table located by the front window.

"Come here often?" Ginger asks.

"Nearly every day."

"Same old Dustin, living on the wild side."

"Yep."

The pain is creeping back with every reference to the past.

"So, what brings you here to the city?" Dustin asks.

"Uh, the championship game," she says with a dumbfounded look.

"Oh, yeah, the championship game."

"You didn't watch it?"

"Yeah, I caught it. I just had a brain lapse." Dustin says, digging down deep for the strength to discuss this topic. "Boy, that's great for Hank."

His stomach turned.

"Yeah! And I think it's going to help me out as well," she says with a gleam in her eye.

"Really, how so, Tank's Tink?"

A scowl quickly formed on her face.

"I hate that name!" she says.

Dustin internally enjoyed delivering that little blow. He knew it wouldn't last long, but he enjoyed it nevertheless. Even though he knew it was wrong, he couldn't resist. After all, he's only human. At least that's his justification.

"So, you see, I got on with the BBC about six months ago. Just as a runner, trying to get my break into broadcasting. Anyway, this sports reporter, Gil, wanted the exclusive with Hank. He promised to help me get my break if I helped him with Hank's interview."

"I'm sure he'll help you with something," Dustin says.

"Thanks, that's what Hank said too!" she replies with an annoyed smirk.

Dustin's stomach turned a little when he realized he shared a common thought with Hank.

"Anyway, Gil said that they are looking for someone to scoop the whole VoLt story."

Dustin quits eating. A cold sweat begins to break out over his body. His face loses its color and Ginger notices.

"What's wrong?" she asks.

"The sandwich doesn't taste right."

"Why don't you take it back?" she asks, motioning to the counter.

"Nah, one sandwich out of 365 sandwiches a year is no big deal."

Reluctantly, Dustin entertains Ginger with her promising new job.

"So, do you have any leads or info on the VoLt thing?"

"No, not yet. Just have to be in the right place at the right time."

Dustin gives her a small smile of understanding while a small headache quickly begins to form in his temple.

CHAPTER 5

The music blares throughout the nightclub, as the only noise louder than the music is the occasional "Knights, Knights, Knights," or the "Tank, Tank, Tank" chants. Members of the Gold Knights filter the popular establishment. Fresh off the victory just two days earlier, the team celebrates in style. Patrons are quick to purchase the sports stars drinks of their choice. And nobody's cashing in better than Hank himself.

A mug in one hand, Tank walks around the bar giving high fives to anybody and everybody. The butt of a cigarette hangs from the corner of his mouth. His eyes droop with drunkenness. He is proudly wearing his navy rugby shirt, all the while being photographed by random photographers.

Ginger sits in the corner of the bar watching the spectacle of a boyfriend take victory lap after victory lap throughout the club.

"Had enough yet?" asks a fellow teammate's girlfriend as she leans over to scream the question in Ginger's ear.

"I know my role."

This is her role, the trophy girlfriend. Ginger watches in slight disappointment at her boyfriend's antics. A blank look comes over Ginger as she begins to space off. It's her only refuge in her current situation.

Ginger started dating Hank just as his college career starting picking up. Back then, she looked for something wild and daring, not safe and sound. Not maturity, but immaturity. That's what captivated her.

Always feeling like the ugly duckling in high school, she didn't really blossom until she reached college. Hank just happened to be one of the first to notice the new girl on campus. Soon, she became the "it" girl on the college grounds. Ginger enjoyed being the envy of all the girls for once in her life. For so many years, she had been passed over by guys in favor of more popular girls. And it didn't end there, she watched roles and positions that she tried out for be given to less appreciative and "prettier" girls. At least she always had Dustin to rely on during those rough teenage years. Always there to talk to when needed, to dance with at dances, and the shoulder she needed to cry on. Always there as a friend, as her rock.

Ginger continues to sit in her seat in the back corner booth, rocking side to side with the beat of the music. She would occasionally look around to find Hank's location, but this time she couldn't find him. She shifts her position and strains her neck to find him. Finally, she locates him speaking to a gentleman she didn't recall seeing before. She studies the interaction of the two from across the club.

Fighting the blaring music, Hank leans down to the man.

"Man, I need more juice!" he shouts in the man's ear.

Seemingly slightly annoyed at Hank's drunken loud whisper, the man puts his hand on his shoulder to create a safe space from the sports' giant.

"Dude, you've won! You don't need it anymore," the thirty-year-old man dressed in black and sporting a black leather jacket says. Cautiously looking around, he runs his hand over his heavily greased black hair.

"Man, Ronnie, I need it!"

"Man, you better be careful. It's just a matter of time before they'll start to detect it."

Hank looks at Ronnie with a "come on" look. After a few seconds pass, Ronnie smiles.

"Okay, Okay. I'll text you when I have it."

"Great, you're the man!"

Hank looks up to see Ginger make her way over to him across the floor, weaving in and out of the crowd.

"Better go," he whispers in Ronnie's ear.

"Gone," Ronnie says as he pats Hank on the shoulder.

Ronnie makes his escape just before Ginger reaches Hank.

"Who was that?" she asks, casually pointing to Ronnie as he walks out of the bar.

"Oh, just a fan. He just kept rambling on. You know, part of the deal. If they buy you a pint, you gotta let them talk your ear off for a while."

"Oh," she pauses. "Are you ready to go?"

"Uh, no!" he answers in a somewhat hateful tone. "Why would I want to leave?"

He stretches out his arms and swivels slightly, displaying the partying atmosphere.

She looks at him with a disappointed look. He gently smiles and asks. "Do you want to go?"

"Yeah," she says, looking pitiful.

"Well, how about you and Susie, Jim's girl, go on home together? I know she's ready to go too."

Ginger sighs.

"Okay, whatever."

"Great!" Tank says as he whistles to Jim, indicating that he found someone to take Susie home.

Susie walks up to Ginger and yells into her ear, "Thanks so much, my head is pounding. I was ready about an hour ago."

Ginger just gives an understanding nod as the two head out the door. Ginger turns around to see Tank not miss a beat of the celebration. Turning back around, Ginger runs right into a large athletic man.

"Pardon me," she said as he places her hand quickly on his chest for buffer effect.

"Oui," answers the man with a heavy French accent. He gently pushes her to the side, as five other men follow him into the nightclub.

Looking at Susie with an embarrassed look, she asks, "Where did they come from?"

Susie just shrugs her shoulders a little, "Don't know, don't care."

Ginger turns around and continues her walk home. She has to run to catch up with Susie. They are about a half block away, when they hear gunfire. They stop and look at each other.

"Did that come from the bar?" Ginger asks.

"I don't know," Susie says as they look back at the nightclub.

Suddenly, they could see patrons running out of the bar. Ducking their heads as a few more gunshots are fired. Ginger and Susie begin running back to the club as they realize that none of the fleeing patrons are members of the Gold Knights. Just as they get there, a body comes crashing through the nightclub's main window.

Susie screams as Ginger holds her breathe. A member of the Gold Knights rolls over on his back, face bloody. Ginger tries to make out the player, but she doesn't recognize him. She attempts to duck down to help the injured player when a large, caped figure leaps down from the top of the nightclub building and lands between the Knight and the shattered window. Then, like a pouncing tiger, the long black caped figure leaps through the establishments' gaping hole.

Ginger turns around to look at Susie, who has a blank stare on her face.

"Wa—wa—was that—" Ginger stammers, pointing to the broken window.

Her mouth hung slightly open and her eyes widen to match Susie's.

"That VoLt thing?" Susie responds, questioning what she saw too.

CHAPTER 6

VoLt sat on all fours on top of the French assailant that had the gun. The first one he went after when he leaped through the window. The gunman was out cold. VoLt stands there staring down the five other men. He looks up to see one of the Knights being laid down carefully on the floor by three of his teammates. Blood seeps through his jersey from a gunshot wound to the abdomen. Two Knights kneel down beside him.

"Hang on, Jim!" one shouts as the music continues to blare. Other patrons are starting to peer back up from whatever cover they took when the gunshots started moments earlier.

One of the French men notices VoLt checking on the wounded man and attacks. The man swings with a baseball bat, hitting VoLt across the back. VoLt lunges forward as the other four French begin brawling with other team players. VoLt growls in pain, quickly turning around to face his attacker head on. The man raises the bat up with both arms and charges at VoLt. The bat equals the reach both of them had. VoLt threw his fist with all his might into the man's chest just as the bat came down. VoLt turns to the side just as the bat lands dead on his hump. The second hit of the bat is not nearly as painful as the first since the attacker lost his grip.

The man falls on his back holding his chest in pain. VoLt picks him up and throws him on the DJ stand, where he crashes down on the stereo system. The impact abruptly turns off the music.

Then VoLt turns around to see a French guy go after another Knight with a chair. The Knight is one of them that had a hold of Jim until they laid him on the floor. VoLt pauses just for a moment, and then leaps across the floor grabbing the chair away from the stoutly built Frenchman. The man turns around only to find himself in the creature's clutch by his throat. Then with his other hand, VoLt places it over the Frenchman's face.

"Repent!" VoLt growls.

VoLt doesn't move as he allows his mystical power to take in the man's evil. After the absorption is completed, the creature tosses him to the side where the Frenchman rolls over in pain. VoLt looks around the nightclub where he sees he has a captivated audience. The uninjured Gold Knights seem to have the other Frenchmen pinned down.

"Hold them till the police arrive," VoLt orders, and the Knights simply nod in shocked understanding.

VoLt turns to the Gold Knight that he had saved from the chair attacker.

"Thanks for your help! I didn't see him coming," Hank says as he looks up slightly at VoLt.

The creature just gives Hank a snarl and mumbles under his breath, "If I had known it was you."

"What?" Hank asks as a quick frown came over his face.

"It's only a matter of time before your team finds out who you really are," VoLt growls lowly, just loud enough for Hank to hear.

Jamerson returns the glare.

VoLt could see a glow of red in Hank's eyes. He knows what he's supposed to do. VoLt's responsibility to his fellow man is to help them break free from the control of sin, but he cannot bring himself to do it. Making Hank's life better does not appeal to him in the slightest.

He turns around only to find Ginger standing in front of him. Susie peeks around Ginger to see Jim lying on the floor.

"Jim!" she cries as she dashes to his side.

Sirens could be heard approaching from the distance. The creature walks past Ginger as she appears to struggle for something to say.

"I'm Ginger Nevine with the BBC. Can I ask you some questions?"

The creature stops and looks at her. She stands completely frozen, eyes wide open as if wondering if he would devour her for merely speaking. He gives a brief snort in her direction, turns, and proceeds out the door. Once VoLt walks out of the nightclub, photographers immediately begin snapping pictures. Feeling caught off guard by the sudden paparazzi, he quickly dashes down the closest alley and leaps out of sight.

Stunned, Ginger stands there motionless. She takes a step in his direction, seemingly with intentions to chase VoLt down. She pauses there for a moment, pondering what she should do. Dropping her shoulders with an exhale, Ginger turns around and rushes back to the bar to aid Jim. Inside, Ginger passes a statue-like Hank. She momentarily glances up at him as he stands motionless looking out the large hole in the window, his brow angled down over his eyes.

"Who is that creep?"

CHAPTER 7

In a dark corner on a rooftop of an apartment building, three blocks from the nightclub, VoLt releases the evil bile by forced vomit. Tasting the anger of the Frenchman, VoLt clears his throat and spits out the remnants. Reaching in his cloak, he pulls out a match, and strikes it against the concrete rooftop causing it to ignite. Dropping it on the bile, he watches as a small ball of fire briefly errupts only to evaporate with a small, whispered hiss.

The capability of cleansing his adversaries of the controlling grip that sin had over their lives was hard for Dustin to wrap his head around. All he knows that it was all God's doing in allowing him to see the red glow of evil in their eyes. It wasn't Dustin himself that judged whether or not these individuals needed cleansing, but God himself. As disgusting as the act was of drawing the sin out only to throw it up later and ignite it to get rid of the evil, Dustin somehow took comfort that God was in control.

This was the first time though that he ever refused to cleanse someone. He knew Hank was a bad person deep down, and seeing the red glow in his eyes only confirmed that. But purposely refusing what God had wanted him to do left him feeling a little guilty inside.

Shaking off a shiver of the moment, the creature walks to the edge of the rooftop, closest to the nightclub. He can hear the commotion still going on below. Aggravation consumes him. The man he cleansed tonight was the very man he saved two nights ago on the night of the championship game. Who's to blame? Who's at fault? Who should pay? Constant questions when he attempts to aid those in need. Did he make a bad decision when he helped those men that night? Dustin would have to remind himself that everyone is susceptible to their own free will. That is something that he does not have control over and it's something that God leaves for everyone to decide for themselves.

But now the voices of doubt begin to arise again, and with the return of Ginger into his life, the voices were getting louder. VoLt crouches down on the rooftop catching his breath as his mind begins to wander back on his past with Ginger and with Hank.

Since the first grade, Dustin and Ginger were inseparable. Growing up in the same neighborhood, where you see one, the other wasn't too far away. They played soccer, hide and seek, house, and war. By the time they grew out of their bikes, the rubber on the tires had nearly wore out, exposing tiny portions of the air tube underneath.

Ginger's name didn't quite suit the tomboy personality that she had. She could hang with the boys in any game. The two had their occasional spats regarding who shot who, who's it, and who's out. But by the time the sun set, all was well.

When they hit junior high though, things began to change. Girls began to turn into women and boys seemingly began to turn into bigger boys. Ginger began hanging out with her girlfriends more. Trendy blouses and designer pants took the place of T-shirts and patched-up jeans. Then came the first day of their freshman year when Dustin saw Ginger for the first time in makeup. Dustin couldn't talk to her for a week. He'd reluctantly watched her transform from his buddy into a person that he could no longer tackle in a pop-up rugby game. She had become delicate and pretty, at least she did in his eyes.

Despite the fact that Dustin recognized her change in appearance, others still saw her as the tomboy who fought for the football or slid into home. That stigma caused her to run home crying or to the shoulder of her best friend on many occasions.

Dustin had his own growing pains as well. At school, he had the personality that allowed him to stay hidden or go unnoticed. Just another face in the crowd, at least that's how he felt. Never the sports star, never the debate champion, never the lead in the play, never the solo in choir or band. Always number two on the role call just after Adams, and always Ginger's friend, but just a friend.

There would be times when she would cry on his shoulder after some boy asked another girl to the dance instead of her. Dustin would often console her and attempt to build her back up.

"What do you even see in him? You deserve someone who will treat you with respect," he said on an occasion or two.

Hoping she would pick up the hint, she would just return with a compliment and say something like, "I wish the other girls saw what I see in you."

That phrase brought such pain to Dustin's heart. It was right there, the opportunity, but not the words. That stupid mental block that kept him from saying what his heart screamed. All Dustin could produce was a small goofy smile.

High school graduation had arrived with classmates hugging other classmates, and telling each other good luck and good-bye. All in all, they survived. Ginger had a boyfriend who she had been dating for a good portion of the senior year. His name was Jake. A transfer student from Sweden, Ginger had been assigned to help him transition to the school system. Their friendship had blossomed and Ginger at long last finally had a boyfriend of her own. But when graduation ended, Jake also ended their relationship. And once again, Ginger came crying to Dustin, and again, he gave her the words of encouragement she needed to hear.

Wiping away the tears and attempting to put on a brave face, she gave Dustin a heartfelt smile and said, "Dustin, you should be in the ministry."

Not exactly the words he wanted to hear. Sure, it seemed like a genuine compliment, but God was the furthest thing in his mind at that moment, and here she was, throwing Him into the mix.

"Lord knows I've given you plenty of training in consoling the hurt," Ginger joked as she blew her nose.

"Oh, I think that should be a calling from up above on something like that."

He looked at her with a smirking grin. She raised an eyebrow.

"Maybe you're just not answering."

Dustin responded with a small laugh as he felt his stomach drop slightly. There were moments where he entertained the thought of going into the ministry. He just didn't think he had what it took. Besides, he didn't want to leave Ginger. He hoped that something might start between them eventually.

That summer, both Ginger and Dustin prepared themselves for college. The night before they left, the two went for a sentimental walk through the neighborhood and fields where they grew up playing. They reminisced over long forgotten games and bike rides. They found themselves under the tree in the open field that had served them well as a base, fort, and a general hangout. Searching the tree, Ginger found the carving that they made years ago.

G -n- D = Friends 4 Ever

"Wow, look at that," she said as she ran her fingers over the carving.

"Yeah," he replied as he touched the portions that her fingers had not covered.

Then, smoothly and softly, he ran his fingers over hers. With a genuine look of surprise, she looked up at him. Her eyes glossed over as finally, Dustin felt that Ginger was at last seeing him in the same way that he had seen her in all those years. They both leaned in and kissed. Soon they embraced and held each other. Her lips tasted better than he had dreamed about. His heart raced, but it raced smoothly.

She pulled back and looked tenderly into his eyes. The words that he wanted to tell her were on the verge of breaking through that wall in his brain.

"Dustin, I can't," she said as she leaned in to rest her forehead on his. "I can't lose you."

"What?" he asked. "Lose me? You can't lose me, I'm right here," he said with a smile.

"No, I can't do this," she paused. "You mean too much to me. I don't want to ruin what we have."

A sudden numbing sensation began to come over Dustin's body.

"Ruin what?"

"This, our friendship. I can't lose my best friend, Dustin," Ginger said as she patted his chest softly.

"Why can't it be more?" he asked.

"Because, I don't know what I want. I don't know what to expect. All I know is that I don't want anything that's weird or confusing."

"Weird or confusing?" he said.

"Now don't take it like that."

Dustin leaned back against the tree, resting his head back, looking straight up into the stars through the maze of branches over their heads.

Ginger sighed at his subtle reaction.

"See, this is what I don't want, this is what I don't need," she said as she stepped back, folding her arms.

"Ginger, I'm dying here. I've wanted nothing more than this."

"Really?" she asked surprisingly. "You've never indicated that before."

Dustin wondered for a moment if it would have made a difference if he did express his feelings for her earlier in their friendship.

"Please, Dustin, I need you, I need your friendship. I need it more than ever. I'm scared out of my mind about college. I need my rock, my friend, my Dustin."

This isn't exactly how Dustin had envisioned it playing out in his head. But if he couldn't be her boyfriend, he might as well be her friend. Besides, things might change at college.

After a moment of purposeful awkwardness, he reluctantly shrugged his shoulders in an understanding manner and lightly punched her arm to let her know that everything was okay. At least that's the face he put on. Inside, a piece of him died.

CHAPTER 8

Shoving the key in the doorknob, he wiggled and turned it until the door unlocked. Dustin opened the door to his dorm room only to find his new roommate sprawled out all over his bed flipping the channels of the television with the remote. The roommate's bags, books, and other random stuff were scattered all over the place.

"Hey," the roommate said as he casually lifted his arm to wave, but that's all the movement he did.

"Hi, I'm Dustin. Your roommate." he said as he stepped over obstacles that covered the pale blue room, shaking his roommate's hand.

"I'm Hank. Make yourself at home," Hank said. He didn't bother to move or assist.

Dustin looked around to find some portion of the small fifteen by twelve foot room to set his stuff down. There, in the corner of the room, he located a spot to set down his suitcase and backpack. Turning around, he surveyed all of Hank's stuff, noticing a lot of soccer gear.

"You play?" Dustin asked, pointing to his equipment.

"Yeah. Here on a scholarship. Full ride," Hank said in a matter of fact tone.

"Great," Dustin said as he turned to shut the door of his new personal prison cell.

VoLt II

Two weeks into the semester, Dustin sat at his desk trying to understand calculus. A knock at the door broke his concentration. Dustin assumed it was another one of Hank's friends stopping by to make an already difficult subject to study nearly impossible. Dustin didn't even bother to move. After the first day, it became obvious that whoever came by to visit was there to see Hank, and Hank alone.

Hank groaned as he rolled off his bed to answer the door, all the while not taking his eyes off the sports report on the television.

"Yeah," Hank said as he opened the door. "Oh, I mean, Hello."

His voice and tone changed instantly at the realization it was someone else instead of the usual list of buddies who came by to visit.

"Yes, is Dustin here?" asked the voice.

Dustin froze and dropped his pencil. He nearly gave himself a whiplash turning his head toward the door making eye contact with Ginger as she peered around Hank's muscular physique to find Dustin somewhere in the room.

"Yeah, I'm Hank!" he said as he invited her in.

"Nice to me you, uh, Hank."

Dustin jumped up and ran over to her.

"Hey, you! It's good to see you!" Dustin said as he gave her a hug.

"So, hey, how's it goin'?" she asked, looking around the room.

"Fine," he said, nodding his head.

Hands shoved in his pocket, he stood there awkwardly in front of the two of them, desperately wanting to be alone in the room with her. Knowing full well that Hank wasn't going anywhere, his mind raced for an alternative.

"Hey, let's go for a walk," he said in an almost frantic tone.

"Oh, okay," she responded.

Dustin quickly grabbed his coat and placed his arm on her shoulder to guide her out of the room.

"Hey, a walk sounds good. I'll join you guys," Hank said.

"Oh, oh, okay. That'll be great," Ginger responded as she looked at Dustin for reassurance that it was okay if Hank tagged along.

Dustin gave a Ginger a small, pitiful smile.

"Yeah, that's fine," Dustin replied.

Dustin quietly let out a sigh that deflated him internally as his shoulders dropped. The three of them strolled around the campus as Hank steamrolled his way through the conversation. Much to Dustin's dislike, Hank and Ginger appeared to hit it off well as they walked and talked nonstop. He did his best to stay with them, but Dustin spent much of that afternoon following his roommate and his best friend, with his hands shoved in his pockets as the cold, lonely, England wind whipped around him.

CHAPTER 9

The end of the first year at college quickly approached. Students were busy enrolling in next year's classes and making dorm room requests. Dustin had been struggling in his classes all year long. He came to college unsure of the degree he wanted to pursue. He hoped that something would "come to him," but none of the classes seemed to jump start anything inside of him. Something was tugging at his heart, but he couldn't pinpoint where it was directing him.

Dustin silently prayed on his way to the counselor's office for his appointment to enroll in new classes. He grew up in the church, participated and served faithfully along the way. His family had been very active in the church, especially after his father died tragically while serving in the military. He was nine at the time. Dustin carried the pain with him every day, but relied on his faith to carry on. Now, the pain was more evident as he longed for a father to give him advice on what he should do. Dustin's feet dragged along the ground as he made his way to the advisor's appointment. Along the way, he prayed to the only father he had.

Dustin just assumed that college was the natural progression for him to go. The feeling of spinning his wheels and wandering aimlessly through his college courses agitated him immensely.

"Dear Lord, please speak to me. Show me the path you want me to follow."

As the wind howled around him, he recalled a previous sermon that he heard at the local church he attended in college.

The pastor made the remark, "The Lord wants us to blaze a trail instead of following another."

Naturally, Dustin believed that sermon was directed at someone else. Meant for someone that was more confident, strong, and, perhaps, blessed with deep pockets.

As he approached the administrative building, he heard a familiar voice come from behind.

"Dustin, Dustin!"

He turned around to see Ginger jogging toward him. She had a smile on her face.

"Hey," she said.

"Hey, whatcha doin'?"

"Oh, I was heading to the library when I saw you. Where are you heading?"

"I'm going to sign up for next year's classes."

"Really? Are you leaning toward anything?"

"No. Just can't seem to find anything that inspires me."

"Just give it time, something will come along."

Ginger paused as she softly bit her lip and tilted her head slightly as if she wanted to change the topic.

"It's funny that I saw you because I was just thinking about you."

"Really?" Dustin smiled.

It always felt good to Dustin to hear Ginger talk like that.

"Yeah, I really need to talk to you about something," she said.

"About what?" he replied with a curious eager look.

"About Hank?" she asked as she twisted slightly, knowing she would be hitting on a tender subject with Dustin.

Dustin's stomach turned a little as he felt his face droop.

Hank had made it known to Dustin on several occasions about what he thought of Ginger. Hank knew Dustin and Ginger were close and had hoped that Dustin might put in a good word on his behalf. That never happened. He just informed Hank that Ginger wasn't his type.

"What about Hank?" Dustin asked as his tone began to change.

"Well, I just wanted to let you know that Hank and I have been dating since Christmas."

Dustin's head began spinning and a cold sweat broke out as his heart began beating rapidly.

"What? Since Christmas? Behind my back?" he responded in a loud tone.

"Dustin, please, hear me out," Ginger said as she tried to console him by softly reaching out and grabbing him by the arm. "I knew this wouldn't be easy. But I didn't like going behind your back either. I needed to tell you."

"You kept this from me for four months! Sounds like it wasn't too hard for you to do."

Dustin slowly moved his arm away from her touch.

"Hey, I feel horrible about this! I wasn't expecting this!" she said.

"What do you want from me?" Dustin asked angrily.

"I just want you to understand. To support me, to forgive me. And most importantly, to be my friend."

"That's all I ever been. I can't say the same about you," Dustin said.

Dustin knew he delivered a harsh blow. Ginger stood there glaring at him. Tears welled up in her eyes. Dustin took a small internal delight in finally seeing her in some kind of pain in which he could take the credit. After all, he had spent many nights heartbroken over her decisions. This one time won't make a difference.

She wiped a tear away angrily from her face and turned and walked away.

Dustin looked up at the administration building. Taking a deep breath, he turned around and went back to his dorm room. For the first time since he arrived on campus, he walked with determination. His mind raced with different scenarios of what he would say to Hank. His blood boiled.

When he reached his room, he swung the door open with force, attempting to make an impressive, offensive entrance. Dustin wanted to catch Hank off guard, but to his disappointment, the room was vacant. Standing there fuming, looking around the room at all of Hank's crap, he struggled to decide on his next move. He wanted to make a statement, even if it fell on deaf ears. That's when Dustin made a decision. He proceeded to pack his things, and left the university forever.

CHAPTER 10

Dustin's mind flashes back to the present as he sits on the rooftop, still watching the glow of the police cars lights flicker in the air in front of the nightclub. The ambulance carrying Jim had left for the hospital. Now the police were just taking notes from the scene. The pain of the fallout with Ginger is still fresh in his mind, despite the fact that five years had passed.

When Dustin left the university, he went home to his mom and grandmother. He cried as he told them about his feelings for Ginger and the revelation of the relationship that had been going on with Hank and Ginger. He informed them that he had been struggling to find the path that was intended for him. He remembered his grandmother standing behind him as he sat at the kitchen table. She placed her hands on his shoulders and made the statement that altered his path and at times haunted his memory.

"My only wish for your dad was for him to either serve in the military or in the ministry."

Those words still ringing in his ears as a slow steady rain began to fall on the city.

"Sometimes it feels like Dad took the easier one," Dustin said as he looked at the gold V medallion.

Now, Ginger and Hank have re-entered his life. Another test from God? He searched for the meaning in their paths crossing again. Dustin had been able to move on. He had to. The teachings at the seminary taught him the importance of forgiveness.

Just like the sermon Jesus taught to the disciples regarding the servant who begged for freedom from the debt he owed to his master. The master showed mercy by wiping the debt clean. But the servant didn't show mercy to the individual that owed him money. When the master found out that the servant did not reciprocate the mercy he received onto others, he had the servant thrown in prison. Dustin had to pass on forgiveness to Ginger and Hank. As hard as it may be, he had to. He knew his very soul may depend on it.

Locating a fire escape, Dustin climbs over the ledge and onto the metal black stair case structure. Making his way down until he reaches the bottom bar, he grabs it and allows his body to fall. Catching his weight, he allows himself to swing back and forth. Releasing his grip, he drops and ends up landing in a puddle that he didn't see until he is right on top of it. Water splashes up and drenches his shoes and pants while splattering up, covering his face.

"Great. Not my night."

CHAPTER 11

The knock at the door wakes Dustin up from his deep sleep. Rubbing his eyes, he looks at the clock. Seven in the morning. He isn't late, so who could be knocking at his door?

"Just a minute," he hollers to the door.

Throwing on a robe, he opens the door to see Pastor Phillips standing there with the *London Times* paper in his hand.

"Rough night last night?" the pastor asks.

"You could say that."

The pastor hands him the newspaper as Dustin studies the picture of his alter ego on the front page.

"Not really my best side," Dustin said, trying his best to ease the tension of the moment.

"Are you all right? The report indicates there were gunshots and that you were hit across the back with a bat."

"It all happened pretty fast. But I'm all right."

Looking over the article, he tries to locate information on the wounded player.

"Does it say how Jim is doing?" Dustin asked.

"Jim?"

"Yeah, that's the name of the Knight that was shot."

"Uh, the TV reports indicate he's in critical condition," the pastor answers.

"TV reports?"

"Yep, you're all over that too. They have this new reporter, Ginger Nevine, all over the BBC," the pastor said.

"Great," Dustin says as he attempts to stretch his arms and back, finally feeling a little soreness from the bat attack.

The two men stood silent, looking at the floor. Knowing full well that this exposure to the press could alter their game plan, their minds race for any possible answers.

The pastor finally broke the quiet awkwardness.

"Okay, I'll let you back to getting dressed and such. I just wanted to make sure you're okay."

"Well, thanks. I'll be up in a bit."

Dustin makes it to the sanctuary to find Pastor Phillips speaking with someone. The individual had her back to him as the pastor looks in his direction with a perplexed look on his face.

"There's Dustin right there," the pastor said motioning back behind her.

The woman turns around and her eyes lit up.

"Dustin! Did you see? Did you see?" Ginger said in an excited voice.

"See what?" Dustin said, trying to play along.

"I got the exclusive on the VoLt thing! He came to the rescue of Hank and his teammates, and it all happened in front of me!"

Pastor Phillips looks wide eyed at Dustin as he finally appears to be putting all the pieces together. The pale face of the pastor indicates that he realizes this Ginger girl is the same girl that Dustin was hung on so badly for years, and now she's the one trying to track down VoLt. It appears to be a little overwhelming for the pastor to take in.

"I'll leave you two alone," the pastor said, giving Dustin a look that he understood. The look he gives Dustin indicates that Phillips would be waiting for a full update on the situation at hand whenever the time would allow it.

Dustin excuses him.

"Dustin, all I had to do was wait for the crew to show up and I had the scoop!"

"Wow, that's great!" he says, showing his enthusiasm for her. "Was anybody hurt?" Dustin asks, trying to get Ginger to calm down a bit.

"Oh, yeah, just one guy, but I think he'll be okay."

A little shocked to hear her coldness toward the wounded soccer player, he tries to understand her excitement.

"So where's Hank?" he asks.

"Oh, he's sleeping still, I think. He didn't come home till late. You know, giving reports. He was crabby though. I don't think he enjoyed the encounter with VoLt as much as I did," Ginger says, rattling on like a machine gun, the adrenaline seemingly still flowing through her body.

"Come on, let's celebrate! My treat!" Ginger says, gleaming with newfound success.

"It's only eight," Dustin replies.

"Then we'll get breakfast! Come on, just you and me. Just like the old times!"

"Okay," he says, giving into her request, just like the old times.

CHAPTER 12

In a luxurious apartment, Ronnie stands in front of the large bay window looking out over Hyde Park. Dressed in designer slacks with a tight white silk shirt and a sharp black tie, he sips on a *cappuccino*. The cell phone rings on Ronnie's belt holster. He plucks it from his hip to look at the screen's caller ID. A smile comes over his face.

"That's my boy!" he says just prior to answering it.

He flips the phone open and answers.

"Tank, my boy! Are you okay?" he asks.

He listens to Hank's response over the phone.

"Yeah, I see. You guys are all over the news again! Second time in forty-eight hours."

Ronnie pauses as Hank explains his reason for the call.

"Okay, really though. I mean, he did show up to help you guys."

Ronnie pauses again while listening to his client's rant.

"Tank, this thing's not human. Be careful what you hunt."

Ronnie shakes his head and rubs his eyebrows as if trying to keep a headache from forming.

"Okay, I got a call from my supplier that they might have something that will knock your socks off, and it's undetected by the current system."

Ronnie shakes his head in slight aggravation, as if realizing the fact that Hank didn't quite understand the importance of Ronnie being able to conduct his business under the radar.

"Hank, listen to me. I had to search long and hard to find the juice that you're using now. And I think it's safe to say that it did its job, right?"

Ronnie nods his head in agreement as it appears that Hank needs more.

"Yeah, yeah, man. As soon as I get it, you'll be the first I call. I don't have a price yet but…"

Ronnie's eyes widen and he sways back a bit at Hank's response.

"Okay, that's good to know. When price isn't a factor, then the skies the limit."

"Okay, man. I'll call you."

Ronnie slaps the phone shut. Standing there, he contemplates his customer's request.

Turning around and looking over his expensively decorated apartment, complete with the most expensive entertainment equipment one could buy, he sighs as he seems to notice how empty it truly is. He glances down at a brochure of the Caribbean on his coffee table. Reaching down, he picks it up and looks over it.

"Man, I'm so close. Just another year and I can call it quits," Ronnie says to himself. "Hopefully this bozo won't blow it for me."

Flipping up his phone again, he returns the call he received yesterday. The phone rings as he waits for the gentleman to answer.

"Hello, Mr. Gustav, this is Ron Griner. You called regarding a new item on the market? Yes, sir, just as you hoped, my client is very interested."

Ronnie pauses as Mr. Gustav speaks on the other end.

"Uh, yes, he's very eager. His encounter with the VoLt monster has him all jazzed up. He doesn't like anyone having the upper hand on him."

His eyes widen as he listens to Mr. Gustav's response.

"Okay, sure, yes, we can meet at noon," Ronnie replies, a little shocked at Mr. Gustav's availability. "Really, the London Science Research building? That's really not low key, is it?"

Ronnie stood silently as he received his orders.

"Okay, okay, I'll see you then. Thank you, sir."

Ronnie again closes the phone. A small hint of sweat forms on his forehead. He loosens the tie around the collar of his neck in a nervous manner.

"The London Science Research Center? Who is this guy?" Ronnie says as he paces back and forth in front of the window.

CHAPTER 13

A prison guard walks up to a secured barred door. He places his ID card in front of the scanner, causing the red light on the pad to turn green. A loud pop sounds at the latch and the guard slides the door open. Walking down the corridor, he glances up at the large gray enclosed structure. The facility has three levels and all looks down on the open walkway. The officer checks each cell that he walks by, checking on the inmates. He stops at one cell and taps on the bars with his night stick.

"Your lawyer's here," the guard said to this inmate.

"Ah, right on time," the inmate replies as he stands from his cot and straightens out his gray prison outfit.

The officer opens the cell door and escorts the inmate back down the corridor and through the gated door.

The officer opens the door to the small conference room and leads the prisoner in and sits him down, then proceeds to handcuff the man to the chair. The guard then looks at the lawyer sitting on the other side of the table.

"He's all yours, Mr. Gustav. You have ten minutes," the guard says.

Mr. Gustav just nods in agreement, not taking his eyes off his client. The guard then closes the door and stands watch outside.

"How are you, Professor Zen?" Gustav asks.

"Oh, the food is horrible and the days are long," Zen answers. "I trust you came by to give me an update."

"Yes, I believe Dr. Irvine finally finished enhancing your Kronog formula."

"Great! I knew, given the proper incentive, Irvine could pull it off," Zen says, mildly gloating. "So, when will we be able to implement the plan?" Zen asks.

"Very soon. Our investors are anxious to pick up where we left off over a year ago. They are eager to build an army of these Kronogs. An army of these would make that small country an instant world power in a blink of an eye."

"Very good. And any sightings of my favorite pet?"

"Yes, in fact, his picture was finally captured last night," Gustav says as he pulls out a copy of the *London Times* and places it in front of Zen to see.

"Ah, there he is," Zen says proudly. "We will meet again, my friend. I guarantee it."

Zen leans back in his chair, holding up the newspaper in front of him.

"So, tell me about our newest protégé," Zen requests.

Gustav smiles and he pulls out another newspaper from three days ago.

"His name, Hank 'the Tank' Jamerson. He's the sports star that won the championship for them."

"Ahh...," Zen responds, enjoying the setup.

"In fact, he had a run-in with VoLt last night. Left quite an impression on him. And not a positive one." Gustav continues, "We've had him juiced up for some time now. Now he's eager for more."

"Perfect, simply perfect!" the professor says, leaning his head back in delight.

CHAPTER 14

Ginger is practically skipping down the sidewalk toward Hank's apartment, located on the north side of the River Thames, not far from Wembley Stadium. The photographers had finally gone home and left the modest neighborhood the chance to get back to normal. She trots up the stairs and uses her key to enter. Hank shares the flat with three other guys, so she introduces herself before fully going in, making sure not to catch his roommates off guard or indecent.

"Hello, it's me, Ginger. You guys up?" she calls out.

No one answers. She walks into the foyer and finds the TV still on in the living room just to the right. Looking around, she locates the remote control and turns it off. She places the remote back down on the table and picks up several empty beer cans and wine bottles off the floor and coffee tables.

"Pigs," she mutters.

Eventually, she carries in the trash can and throws away all the empty cans and uneaten pizza as it sat there attracting flies.

"Disgusting!"

She bags up the trash and carries it through the kitchen in the back and out the back door, tossing it in the already overflowing trash dumpster.

"It's a wonder these boys can dress themselves for a game," she says.

She walks back through the house and quietly walks up the stairs to the bedroom. She knocks softly on Hank's door.

"Hank, you in there?"

No answer. She knocks again, this time slowly opening the door. He usually keeps the room nearly pitch black. Just a faint glow of daylight seeps in around the black curtains.

"Hank?" she says as she reaches over and feels the bed. It's empty. She turns around and flicks on the light. The bed hadn't been touched. Frowning and looking around the room for any possible hint where Hank could be. She turns around and walks across the hallway to Devin's room. She taps on the door.

"Devin? Devin, you in there?"

A couple of seconds pass when an exhausted Devin answers.

"Yeah, come in," he says.

She slowly peeks in not knowing what to expect. Devin lies in bed, his sheets covering up to his waist.

"Hey, Gin, what's up?" he asks as he rubs his head.

"Have you seen Hank?"

Devin sits still for a second. Then a regretful look comes over him.

"I'm sorry, Gin, but he didn't come home last night. I figured he crashed at your place last night, ya know."

"No, I didn't see him at all yesterday. I worked most of the day and night," she said, accounting for her whereabouts.

"Man, I don't know what to tell you, girl," Devin paused. "Can I do anything?"

"No, no, thanks. Sorry to bother you," she says as she closes the door.

She stands in the hallway looking into Hank's empty bed. She chews on her fingernails as she looks over his room, then she abruptly stops and lets out a forced breath. The creases on her forehead indicate her frustration and fear regarding Hank's whereabouts. Tears began to fill the lower portion of her eyes as she runs down the stairs and out the door.

In the basement of Berthel Church, Dustin conducts his weekly Bible study class with his students. The studying portion had concluded, and now they were enjoying an old Bible book challenge. Cameron, Abbey, and Kevin stand in front of the class, hands on their Bibles with their thumbs poised to begin the search once the book is called.

"Okay, ready?" Dustin states. "The book is… Leviticus!"

Several of the students cheer on the three contestants as they feverishly thumb through their Bibles.

Cameron rapidly scans through his until he finds Leviticus.

"Found it!" Cameron shouts as Abbey and Kevin look at Cameron in frustration as they both dropped their Bibles to their sides.

"Crud, Cam! Can you sit one out?" Kevin asks with a defeated smile on his face.

Dustin laughs at the exchange amongst his fellow players.

Smiling, Cameron goes to sit by a new member of the class, a young lady named Jayden. Pale and thin and wearing mostly black attire, she seems rather smitten by Cameron he takes a seat next to her after his victorious round. Dustin could tell Cameron was smitten by her as well.

The awkwardness that the two teenagers shared, as well as their attempt to hide their mutual feeling for each other, made Dustin chuckle inside.

"Cam's the man!" shouts the voices of a couple of teenagers in the group.

Cameron flushes with embarrassment at the congratulatory remarks. Dustin reaches over and rubs Cameron's head in a supportive gesture.

"All right," Dustin said as he excuses the two other players to take their seats. "I need three more."

He looks over the classroom and picks out three new players for the Bible game, one of the contestants being Jayden. The three teenagers walk up to the front of the class and hold out their Bibles in front of them. Jayden awkwardly holds the Bible, as if she's never held a book before.

"Uh, I'm not very good at this," Jayden says.

She smiles a painful smile as she lifts up the Bible in front of her, appearing to examine the thickness of the book she holds in her hands.

"Don't worry, you'll be fine," Cameron replies to her softly.

"Okay, ready? The book is…First Timothy!" Dustin smiles as he watches the players quickly thumb their way through their Bibles.

After a couple of seconds, a light brown-haired teenage girl jumps up.

"Found it!" she yells.

Jayden's shoulders drop. She quickly makes her way back to her chair next to Cameron.

"See. I have no business being here," she says, slouching into the seat.

She folds her arms tightly in a protective matter. Cameron places his hand on her shoulder and wiggles it, trying to sooth her feelings.

"Just a silly game," he says, trying to smile through her disappointment.

"I don't fit in here, Cameron. I told you I wouldn't," Jayden replies quietly.

Cameron looks over at Dustin, but Dustin seems to be unaware of the disconnect she has with the group.

"Good job, Grace!" Dustin says, laughing along with the other class members.

"Oh, I was so close!" one of the other players says.

"Close but no cigar!" Grace responds.

Cameron starts to fidget a little in his chair as he seems to be feeling the stress and uneasiness that Jayden appears to be feeling. He keeps glancing back and forth trying to get Dustin's attention without getting the entire class' attention.

Unable to detect Cameron's concern, Dustin stands up and excuses the two from the latest round. As he looks over the class for three new contestants, he recognizes a person standing in the back.

"Ginger?" he asks skeptically, realizing that she appeared to be upset.

He makes his way back to her as the class watches on.

"Everything okay?" Dustin asks.

"I don't think so, I haven't heard from Hank for two days now. He didn't even come home last night."

"Go ahead and have a seat here," he says as he clears off a chair for her.

"We're wrapping this up anyway."

"Dustin, I'm sorry I didn't mean to interrupt your class. I can come back—"

"No, no. It's all right," Dustin says as he tries to comfort her, rubbing her shoulder lightly.

"Hey, guys, I think we'll call it an evening," he says to the group of teenagers. "Thanks again for showing up tonight. Remember, we'll start diving into Revelations next week," Dustin says as the students gathered their belongings and begin to leave.

"Great," Cameron mumbles under his breath, realizing that Dustin seems to be preoccupied with this woman.

Then, Cameron glances back at the woman, as if recognizing her from somewhere.

Jayden stood behind Cameron as Kevin came up beside him.

"Hey, Cam. Is that the lady that's been on TV, talking about VoLt?" Kevin asks.

"Yeah!" Cameron replies as if the answer finally popped in his head. "Yeah, that's her."

Curiosity seems to have gotten the best of Kevin as he slowly approaches Ginger and asks, "You're the one that reported on VoLt, aren't you?"

"Yes, thank you," she says as she greets Kevin with a hand shake. Something about the question seemed personal. "Have you encountered the creature?" she asks cautiously.

"Yeah, nearly two years ago. He, uh, made quite an impact."

Kevin glances over to Cameron and looks around the room as if indicating he wouldn't be here if it wasn't for that encounter.

Ginger looks around the room and sees the same look in Cameron as Jayden stands behind him, almost trying to hide.

"Have you seen this creature too?"

"Yes, ma'am," Cameron says, nodding in agreement.

"Wow," Ginger says in amazement as she looks at the two teenagers. She seemingly forgot why she came here in the first place.

Dustin begins to feel a slight uneasiness with the direction of the conversation.

"That's quite a coincidence that you two have seen it," Ginger says as she glances back between the two.

"Ginger, this is Kevin, Cameron, and…" Dustin says, gesturing to Jayden, waiting to hear her answer.

"This is Jayden," Cameron said, introducing her.

"Well, it's nice to meet you guys," Ginger replies.

Cameron's shoulders dropped, indicating that he had hoped for more attention to the new class member that he introduced, but he could tell by Dustin's reaction that he seemed to be more intrigued with the reporter and the business that brought her here.

"They're my core of the class." Dustin says, gesturing to Kevin and Cameron.

"Wow," she says as she looks at each one. "I'd love to talk to you guys about your encounter with the VoLt thing."

Her eyes widen, as if realizing the potential for an exciting TV interview.

"He's not a thing, he's a caring creature under all that hair and muscle," Abbey says, entering the conversation.

Dustin felt touched to have Abbey defend VoLt, yet the uneasiness grows as the conversation begins to get a little too close for comfort.

"Really?" an intrigued Ginger asks.

"All right, you guys better be going. I don't want you all getting into trouble," Dustin says as he tries to excuse them.

"Hey, Dustin," Cameron replies as he tries to divert Dustin's attention. "I wanted you to meet my friend, Jayden."

Dustin has a bit of difficulty switching gears in his mind. He looks at Cameron and then finally looks at Jayden who seems to be a bit standoffish.

"It's nice to meet you, Jayden," he replies.

"Thanks, nice to meet you too," Jayden replies, but Dustin begins speaking before she could complete her sentence.

"I hope you come back next week!"

"Oh, well, I don't—"

"Cameron, you'll have to work on that," Dustin says with a smile and pats Cameron's shoulder.

"Uh, yeah," Cameron responds with an uneasy chuckle.

Cameron looks over at Jayden who is looking back at him with uneasy eyes as well.

"Okay, nice to meet you, ma'am," Kevin says as he pats the shoulder of Cameron, letting him know they better leave the two alone.

"See ya next week," Kevin says as the four of them exit the room.

Dustin waits until they were out of sight. Then he makes the difficult change of gears in his head as he has to focus on his least favorite subject in the world.

"Okay, what happened to Hank?" Dustin asks.

Dustin could see Ginger shifting the mental gears in her head as well from VoLt back to Hank with her change in facial expression.

"I haven't heard from him. It's not like him. He usually checks in with me at some point during the day."

"He checks in with you?"

"Okay, maybe I check in on him, but I can't find him. I don't know what to do," she says as she buries her face in her hands with frustration, but then she abruptly lifts her head and folds her arms in a guarded manner as if protecting herself from the possibilities of Hank's situation.

"When's the last time you saw him?" he asks.

"At the night club, the other night. I started working once the news crew showed up and he left to be questioned by the police about the fight and shooting. I've looked everywhere. I didn't know who to turn to, until I thought of you," she says with the same pitiful droopy eyes that Dustin had seen on numerous occasions.

"You look tired, go home and try to get some sleep."

"I can't sleep right now," she argues.

"Gin, you're not doing yourself any good wandering around upset like this. Just go home and I'll see if I can track him down somewhere," Dustin replies.

"You would do that for me?" Ginger asks.

"Well, yeah, but remember, Hank and I don't really hang out in the same places."

"Dustin, this means a lot to me."

"Hey, that's what friends are for, right?" Dustin says with a slight bit of sarcasm barely detectable.

"Thanks, Dustin."

Dustin walks Ginger to the subway system while she tells him of Hank's favorite hangout spots. He watches her go past the subway turnstiles and down the arched, white-tiled tunnel to the subway platform. Just as she was about out of sight, she turns and waves. Dustin returns the wave, then turns around and heads back to his quarters.

CHAPTER 15

VoLt crawls out of his secret entrance from his hideout and onto the Underground subway tracks. He runs down the corridors, dodging trains and leaping onto others as he travels south in the direction of Hank's popular hangouts. VoLt had to admit, he could care less what Hank had been up to or where he had been. But nonetheless, here he is, running through sewers and climbing out of manholes looking for the person he probably despised more than anyone.

Knowing it was wrong to feel this way about someone, he just couldn't help but dislike the guy. And in his mind, he felt justified in holding so much hatred toward Hank. Perhaps, he would find Hank in a position that would give him the ammunition he needed to confront Ginger. Maybe Ginger would finally see Hank for who he truly is. He wanted to prove Hank as the malicious lying fraud that Dustin had come to know during his first year in college.

Dustin saw firsthand the parade of women that would come by to visit their college dorm room. He witnessed Hank's egotistical nature to do whatever he could to promote himself over his fellow teammates. Then Dustin helplessly watched as Hank took his best friend from him.

Bar after sports bar, VoLt did not see anything. He had been scouting the nightclubs for nearly four hours when a luxury car catches his attention. As he stands on top of the rooftop, he begins to focus on the silver Mercedes. The shiny car stuck out against the dungy dark street outside the "Sports Spot" club. He watches as the driver gets out and walks to the back door and opens it, allowing the passenger to get out. VoLt assumes it would be another sports celebrity of some sort, but instead, his heart begins to pump rapidly as he recognizes the figure stepping out.

"Gustav!" VoLt growls as he poises himself to pounce on the man who has eluded the police for over a year now. Just as he prepares to jump, he sees Hank come out of the club with another man in a sharp three-piece suit. VoLt freezes as he strains to listen to their conversation.

"Mr. Gustav, I'd like you to meet the Tank, Hank Jamerson," Ronnie proudly introduces his client.

"Nice to meet you, young man," Gustav says.

"Thanks," Hank answers cautiously.

"Hank, Mr. Gustav is going to take care of you," Ronnie says.

"Hey, Ronnie, I prefer working with you," Hank responds as he judgingly looks over Gustav who stands a good foot shorter than him.

"Hank, trust me, you're in good hands," Ronnie says, trying to reassure him by patting Hank on the shoulder.

Gustav walks to the back door of the silver car and gestures for Hank to climb in.

"It's okay, Mr. Jamerson, all your desires will be met," Gustav says.

Hank pauses for a moment with his hands on his hips.

"I don't know," Hank said.

"It's up to you, Mr. Jamerson," Gustav replies. "You can continue using the same stuff that he's been providing you, or you can start using this new formula that will take you to the next level. No one will be able to touch you."

"No one?" Hank asks.

"Like I said, no one."

Hank begins walking to the car when a dark figure lands on the trunk of the Mercedes and then pounces onto Mr. Gustav, causing him to land on his back. The driver quickly grabs the small walkie talkie inside his suit pocket and yells, "Release them! Now!"

"Them?" VoLt asks himself in response to the driver's request.

Ronnie turns and runs down the street with Hank watching in awe as VoLt picks Gustav up with one arm and slams him into the old brick building behind him. Hank then witnesses the creature begin to place his right hand over Gustav's face when two dog-like humans attack VoLt from behind, seemingly coming from out of nowhere.

"Kronogs?" Hank asks himself, as if he recalls information he heard in a news report over a year ago.

One kronog attempts to hold VoLt's arms behind him as the other kronog delivers a couple of blows to his gut. Dazed and in pain, Gustav gets up and grabs Hank and pushes the large sport star easily into the car.

"Go, go, go!" shouts Gustav as the driver quickly jumps back in behind the wheel and speeds away in the now heavily damaged car.

Anger flows through VoLt as he realizes that Gustav is getting away, again. Turning the rage into energy, he breaks free of the kronog, quickly spinning around and putting the creature in a headlock and ramming the kronog's head into the brick wall. The creature goes limp as VoLt throws him to the ground. Then he turns his attention to the other dog-like beast.

The kronog stands on all fours as it rears up its hind legs waiting for VoLt's next move. VoLt roars as the kronog growls back with drool dripping from its jaw. VoLt takes a step toward it when the kronog leaps in the air, landing on VoLt and biting him on the shoulder. Grimacing in pain, VoLt grabs the creature by the neck and flings it to the ground where it lands hard on its back. The creature yelps in pain as VoLt reaches down and yanks off the collar allowing the beast to turn back into its human form. Then, he walks over and rips the collar off the other kronog as well. VoLt stands there looking at the two as they lay on the ground. He doesn't recognize them. Suddenly he hears a vehicle start up further down the nearly pitch black alley. VoLt looks up to see a dark-colored van drive off. He strains to read the license plate number as it speeds away.

"Now where did they come from?" VoLt quietly asks himself.

One of the attackers begins to move around just as people start to file out of the bar. VoLt quickly grabs him and flings him over the shoulder and escapes. The man begins to scream at the realization of being in VoLt's clutch.

A couple of pedestrians stop and look down the alley where the screaming originates. Some gasp at the sight of the infamous creature with the would-be victim in his grasp. They stand still as they watch the monster slip into the darkness along with the cries of help.

"Did you see that? That VoLt thing took someone with him," one patron says.

"Yeah, do you think he's going to eat him?" asks another.

"Someone better call the police," another says as he walks over and bends down to aid the unconscious man on the ground.

"Man, I'm getting back inside before he comes back," another bar patron says as the majority of the group went back into the nightclub. Others stay out, waiting on the police after hearing the distant sirens approach the scene.

CHAPTER 16

Under a dark bridge, VoLt drops his attacker on his back. He reaches up and grabs his injured shoulder. A quick assessment tells him it's more than just a scratch.

"Who are you?" VoLt barks.

"Don't hurt me!" the man cries.

"I'm not! Who are you?" he asks again.

"My…my name is Paul."

"How did you get acquainted with Gustav?"

"Who?"

"Gustav."

"I, I, I don't know, I work maintenance at the LSRC. We were at work and on a break when this guy entered the break room and started up a conversation with us. Later he offered me and Mick a cup of coffee. We took it and the next thing I know is that I'm down here with you."

"LSRC?"

"London Science Research Center," Paul answers.

"So you don't know the man who did this to you?"

"No, no idea. That place is full of doctors. He could have been one of them. All I know is that I just want to go home," Paul says as he shakes in cold and fear.

VoLt bends down to look at the man face to face. He doesn't see a red glow of evil in the man's eyes. Paul

VoLt II

appears to be telling the truth. Somehow, Gustav has devised a formula that turns unwilling participants into deranged, mind-controlled, dog-like creatures.

VoLt looks down at Paul who sits on the ground in his ripped, navy blue maintenance uniform. He's curled up in a ball, rocking back and forth.

"Then you better go home," VoLt says in a tone that brings some peace to Paul as he realizes he is free to go.

"What are you going to do?" Paul asks as he stands up.

"I guess I need to pay the doctor a visit," VoLt answers as he rubs his wounded shoulder.

"Well, please do it on my day off," the maintenance man requests.

The Mercedes pulls in to the service garage of the London Science Research Center. The driver parks behind a couple of delivery trucks. Mr. Gustav and Hank step out of the car. As they walk away from the car, Hank glances back surveying the damage to the trunk lid.

"Man, that beast tore it up," Hank says.

Gustav seems the least impressed with VoLt's handiwork.

"So, you're telling me that this VoLt thing is a person, he just has this ability to transform into that thing?"

"Precisely," Mr. Gustav replied, motioning Hank over to the elevator doors.

Hank keeps looking back at the heavily damaged car.

"How did he get this ability?"

"By accident," Gustav answers, "but we think we found a formula that will generate enough strength and energy that could match his strength if needed, except better looking."

"Cool." Hank said. "I'd like to see that test subject."

Gustav smiles slightly.

The elevator stops and the doors open to an extremely sterilized hallway that gleams with shiny white tile flooring and stainless steel walls. Hank follows Mr. Gustav down the bright corridor.

Hank's nose twitches with the pungent sting from the cleaning formula that lingers in the hallway.

"So, is this a government-funded project?" Hank asks jokingly, looking around the various offices they pass.

"You could say that," Gustav answers.

"What government?" Hank asks with a wrinkled forehead.

"Not yours," Gustav answers coldly.

Gustav opens the door to office 10-G. Passing through the secretary's station, they enter the laboratory. The office lab is momentarily vacant, until they hear the service elevator arrive on the floor. The door opens and a frazzled Doctor Irvine steps out. Realizing that he had guests, he straightens out his lab coat and quickly crosses the floor to greet them.

"Tank Jamerson, it's an honor to meet you!" the doctor says with a hint of anxiety.

"Thanks," Hank replies with a skeptical eyebrow raised.

"Uh, thank you for agreeing to test out this new sport formula. I think it will greatly enhance your ability," Irvine stammers a little as he tries to regain his composure.

"Oh, okay," Hank said. His tone indicates a hint of embarrassment for his need to cheat to be competitive. "I just need a little something extra, you know?" Hank said, trying to explain himself.

Mr. Gustav stands silent, watching Doctor Irvine nervously prepare for the experiment.

"Is everything all right, Doc?" Hank asks of the apparent mindset of Irvine.

"Oh, oh, yes. Not a worry," the doctor said, clearly aware of his emotional state. "Just excited to meet such a celebrity. Now, if you could just lay down here, we'll prep you."

Irvine guides Hank to the lab gurney.

"Prep me? Can't you just stick me and go?"

"To fully follow your progress, we need to make sure everything is professional," Irvine explains. "Now, if you could just remove your shirt, we can get started."

"Oh, okay," Hank says as he takes off his rugby shirt and lies down on the cold lab table.

Gustav and Irvine glance at each other after quickly eyeing the impressive physique of Jamerson. Their eye contact indicates that they hadn't expected such a fine specimen for this experiment.

"Whew!" Jamerson whistles as his bare back torso comes in contact with the cold metal gurney.

The doctor takes Hank's arm and locates a strong vein. Then after swabbing his arm with an alcohol pad, he takes the syringe and holds it up to double check the amount of fluid he is prepared to inject in Hank's arm.

"This might sting a little," Irvine warns as he sticks the needle in Hank's vein.

Hank winces in pain.

"Dang, that stuff burns!" Hank says as he grits his teeth.

Then Hank looks around once as his eyes appear to become heavy rather rapidly. He tries to shake his head to stay awake, but the strength of the anesthesia proves to be too strong as he soon finds himself drifting off to sleep.

"Okay, he's ready now," the doctor says, looking at Mr. Gustav.

Gustav rubs his chest, smoothing his gray Italian suit.

"Very well. Let's proceed."

CHAPTER 17

Dustin crawls from behind his dresser and slides it back to conceal the secret door. He takes off his black woolen cloak and reluctantly examines his injury.

"Oh, crud," he says as he realizes the severity of his injury. "I don't want to go to the bloody hospital for this."

He bends down and pulls out a first aid kit that Pastor Phillips insisted he keep, just in case of times like this. Opening the kit, he pulls out the small bottle of rubbing alcohol and a large gauze packet. Pouring the alcohol on the gauze pad, he holds his breath as he gently dabs the wipe on the wound. The alcohol burns as it makes contact. Dustin grabs his bed cover and squeezes it with all his might. After the burning sensation finally subsides, he creates a makeshift large bandage using gauze and tape and places it over his shoulder.

Dustin sits there for a moment, trying to assess all the information he gained tonight. He discovered that Hank had been using some kind of steroid formula to increase his physique and ability. In the year that they roomed together in college, he knew that Hank had been using steroids but he didn't want to come across as a snitch and become a hated man on campus for blowing the would-be star's climb to greatness. As much as he wanted to take Hank down from his mighty perch, that small still voice echoed in his ear.

"It's not our place to judge others."

Knowing from where the small voice resonated, he realizes that Hank would ultimately pay for his deception and lies when God will bring whatever justice is needed. But Dustin also knows it would be in God's own time. Deep down, Dustin had always hoped that maybe he would be around to witness it.

Now though, the time seems right to bring his own justice down on Hank. Dustin finally has the proof to tell Ginger the truth about Hank. The moment he longed for had arrived. Dustin tries to envision how he could tell her. He entertains the scenario of delivering the shocking news to Ginger and being there to sweep in and save the day. Then, a guilty feeling comes over him that he recognizes.

He kneels at his bed and prays.

"Dear Lord, forgive me for entertaining the notion of vengeance on my part. I serve you, Lord. Vengeance is yours, not mine. Continue to guide me down the path you have put before me. Give me strength to fight the urges that would bring false pleasure. For in your name I pray. Amen."

Some prayers were hard to say. He didn't know if this prayer was full hearted or not. He realizes that it is a prayer that he knows he should pray, even though his heart may not be in it. Dustin stands and walks over and turns off the light and then tenderly, he crawls into bed.

Letting out a sigh of relief, and taking deep breaths, he finds himself quickly falling asleep.

Cars line up in front of the building that houses the BBC. Most of them are television vans, gassed up and ready to go at a moment's notice. Dustin trots across the shiny flat concrete entrance into the lobby of the station. He locates the receptionist and makes his way to her. She looks up and greets him with a smile.

"Good morning! Welcome to the BBC. Can I help you?" she asks.

"Uh…" Dustin mutters as he glances around, looking at one of the four flat screen televisions placed in each corner of the lobby.

To his surprise, he recognizes the individual on the television.

"Yes, I'm here to see her," he says as he points to the woman giving the report on the television. The footage is a couple of days old as it is recapping a story on VoLt.

"Oh, Ginger Nevine? Do you have information regarding the VoLt phenomenon?" the receptionist asks.

The question takes Dustin by surprise. He quickly thinks about the information he did indeed have regarding VoLt. Then the word "phenomenon" bounces around in his head. As if VoLt is a phase or a fad.

"No, I'm an acquaintance of hers."

"Is she expecting you?"

"I don't believe so," Dustin answers.

"Okay, if you don't mind, please take a seat and I'll see if I can reach her," she said, gesturing to the long bench that ran along the front window.

"Thanks."

He sits down for a few moments when he sees Ginger come running down the smooth concrete stairs into the lobby. She looks frantically around. It appears she had been in the makeup department because she still had the tissue around her neck. Ginger scans the lobby until she locates a familiar face.

"Oh, Dustin. It's you," she says with a slight hint of disappointment.

"Sorry to bother you here," he says as he realizes who she hoped to find. Needless to say, her greeting isn't the most uplifting to Dustin's ears as he slowly pulls himself off the lobby bench.

"Did you find him?" she eagerly asks.

"No, I'm sorry."

Ginger sighs as her shoulders drop.

"Where could he be?"

Dustin fought with all his might to keep from telling her what he knew.

"He'll turn up somewhere, I'm sure of it," Dustin replies. He could feel a sense of guilt come over him, much like the feeling he had when he didn't tell Miss Parsons everything about his first initial meeting with Tim Warner. But he knew deep down he had to protect her at the time.

"What if that VoLt thing got him? We have witnesses that claim he carried someone off last night on the south side of London. That could have been Hank?"

"I don't think he's that kind of person," Dustin answers, slightly offended by her accusations.

"You don't know that!" she snaps back.

Dustin doesn't say a word. He just raises his eyebrows in disbelief of her claim.

"I'm sorry, Dustin, I don't mean to be short, I just…" she begins to cry as she reaches out for Dustin.

He steps in and holds her as she cries into his shoulder like she had done on so many other occasions.

"I don't believe it!" shouts an angered voice behind them.

They both turn around to find Hank halfway between them and the front door.

"I'm gone for two days, and this little twerp is trying to squeeze his way in!" Hank barks as he turns around and bolts out the thick glass door. He pushes the door with such force that it slams against the building's front wall of glass. Everyone in the lobby stops and stares as Hank continues to storm down the sidewalk.

"Hank!" Ginger says loudly as she quickly releases Dustin and runs out the door after Hank.

Dustin slowly walks out, feeling a hint of embarrassment as the receptionist and other onlookers watch the drama unfold in front of them. He watches as Ginger runs out of the door and catches up with Hank.

"Hank, Hank! Stop, please! You don't understand, when I couldn't find you, I went to Dustin to help me find you."

Hank looks at Ginger with a disgusted look. "I don't need to be found!"

"Well, I was concerned, Hank. That's not like you!" she pleads.

"I'm fine! At least I was till I saw you with him!"

Hank points in Dustin's direction. Dustin stops and stands back as Hank accuses him of trying to steal his girl. Inside, Dustin couldn't believe what he was hearing. The fact that Hank saw Dustin as a threat brought a microscopic sense of joy. Almost as soon as he felt the elation of the moment, a small voice told him not to take delight in other's misery. Dustin wishes he had a way to mute that small whisper.

"I don't trust that little twerp," Hank continues the verbal attack.

"Baby, come on. Dustin's harmless. We just wanted to know where you were."

Dustin stands there with all the ammo he needed to shut him up. The urge grew inside him to finally call him out for what he truly is. He approaches Hank and Ginger as the adrenaline flowed.

"Hank, she's telling you the truth. She wanted me to help find you. That's it. I just came by here today to let her know I didn't find you," Dustin explains as he returns the glare back to Hank.

"Whatever," Hank says as he storms off.

Ginger stops and looks at Dustin and mouths, "I'm sorry." Then she turns and follows Hank. Dustin watches as she chases him down. He couldn't understand. If anybody should be mad, it should be Ginger. But somehow, Hank had her apologizing to him. Dustin shrugs his shoulders and heads back home, defeated again.

CHAPTER 18

Evening begins to fall on the city as Dustin walks down the sidewalk toward the church. He holds a small bag of groceries with his left arm while he munches on an apple with his right, enjoying the peace and quiet of the evening. The past couple of nights have been busy for him, and now he relaxes with a nice little stroll. As he approaches the church, he recognizes a figure sitting on the front step. The figure stands up as soon as Dustin reaches the steps. Once again his eyes see Ginger.

"Hey," Dustin says as he walks up the stairs, using a flat monotone.

"Hey," she says with a small smile.

"Everything go okay with Hank?" he asks as he stands two steps down from her.

He intentionally leaves a noticeable barrier of space between them. It's the only defense he could muster up at the moment.

"Not really. I'm just tired of it all," she says as she shrugs her shoulders.

"Tired of what?"

"Mainly him. At first, the wildness was fun. The nonstop parties, the games, the recognition on campus we would get. But he never grew out of it. I tried to focus on his success to overlook his obnoxious, immature ways, but it's constantly about him. It just gets old. Really old," she says as she rolls her eyes.

"Oh, man. I'm sorry, Ginger."

He's not, and wonders if she knows that too.

"And finally my career is starting to take off. Do you think he's supportive?" she asks the rhetorical question. "Absolutely not," she continues as she pushes the air out with her hands. "I just need to focus on my career now."

"Yeah," Dustin says of the irony. Little did she know that Dustin is the reason that her career is taking off.

"Let's go inside so I can put these away," Dustin says.

Ginger sits at the table as she watches Dustin put away his groceries in the kitchen, located in the front portion of the church basement.

"Does Hank know that you're having doubts?" he asks.

"I don't think he cares," she answers as she fidgets with her fingers.

Ginger looks around the kitchen and then over the large dining area.

"So, how long do you plan on staying here?" Ginger asks.

"Oh, I don't know. It's pretty sufficient right now."

Ginger smiles at Dustin.

"What?" he asks with a cautious grin.

"Nothing, it's just…you, you haven't changed a bit," she says. "I mean, you found this calling and you're doing well at it obviously, and yet, you're still the same old you."

"Well," Dustin responds as he hears so many arguable facts in her assessment of him.

"No, really, you're still you." She stands up and walks over to him and gives him a hug.

Dustin didn't anticipate this. He wants to brush her off like she had done to him mentally so many times over the years. Instead, he can feel the barrier start to crumble down as he returns the embrace.

As she holds him, she asks, "You remember that night before we left for college?"

"Yes," he answers.

"Believe it or not, I often wonder what would have happened if we did, you know, date."

Dustin didn't say anything.

"I mean, at the time, I wanted excitement, adventure, fun. I didn't want safe and secure."

"I recall the conversation," Dustin says coldly as the words still stung after all these years. He could feel his embrace weaken.

"And I'm sorry, but I think you are what I needed all along. I was just stupid back then," she continues to hold him as they slowly rock back and forth as they lean against the kitchen counter.

All those emotions flood Dustin's mind. The pain still so evident, and yet, for so long, this is all he wanted. He wanted to tell her everything, but he held back. Instead, the minister in him spoke up.

"We better be careful. We don't want to get caught up in the moment."

Ginger leans back and pats his chest. "You're right."

Just then, Dustin hears someone behind them clear his throat. Panic instantly settles in as a sweat spontaneously beads on his temples. He holds his breath as he dreads looking around to see who had caught them in this semiprivate vulnerable position.

In embarrassment, he looks at the individual and feels a bit of uneasiness when he spots Cameron standing in the kitchen door. Still embarrassed, but not near as severe if it had been Pastor Phillips catching them.

"Oh, hey, Cam. What brings you by?" Dustin asks, feeling his face flush red.

"Sorry to drop by like this, but—"

"No problem. What's up?"

Cameron appears to be very uncomfortable with the situation. Hands shoved in his pockets as he looks down at the ground, unable to look Dustin in the face.

"It's about my friend, Jayden."

"Yeah, the young lady you brought to Bible study, right?"

Dustin carefully steps away from Ginger to meet Cameron halfway in the kitchen.

"Right. Well, you see, she's in some trouble. And she doesn't know how to get out of it."

"What kind of trouble?" Dustin asks.

The rush of embarrassment starts to subside.

Ginger appears to be moderately proud of Dustin and his ability to handle the very parent-like situation. She stands silently but supportive behind him.

"It's hard to explain, but I feel if things don't turn around for her soon, she could be lost forever," Cameron answers through quivering lips.

"Okay, do you know where she is right now?"

"No, I don't."

Dustin could see the desperation in his eyes. Cameron had been a loner for the better part of the year and half that he had known him, and the look on his face indicated that Cameron wasn't sure how to feel or conduct himself. It became evident that Cameron was leaving himself vulnerable to be hurt by someone who he had recently started caring for.

Dustin knew that situation all too well.

"I tell you what, let's meet back here tonight, say, around seven. Then we'll see what needs to be done. Will that be okay?"

"Yeah, yeah, that'll be fine. Thanks, Dustin." Cameron replies. "Sorry again to interrupt you guys."

He gives them a small wave to excuse himself as he makes his way across the dark basement floor and up the stairs and out of sight.

"Whew, that was close," Ginger says with an ornery smile.

"Yeah, a little too close."

"What if that would have been the pastor?" Ginger asks as her eyes lit up with excitement.

"I don't want to think about it."

Dustin feels a little unraveled at being caught in the moment with Ginger by Cameron.

"So, what are you and Cameron going to do regarding his little friend? Going to put on capes and mask and search the alleys for her?

A sudden flush of heat races up his spine.

"Yeah, something like that."

She leans in and gives him one last hug. "Care to walk me home?"

"Sure," he says with a smile.

CHAPTER 19

Using his new badge, Hank swipes it through the door scanner to gain access through the dock door of the LSRC building. He smirks at the badge as he enters the receiving area. No one is around other than the retired cop that serves as the midnight security. Hank just nods and flashes his ID as they pass each other. The guard simply nods an acknowledgement back to him.

Reaching the elevator, he pushes the service button and waits a moment for the elevator to arrive. The doors slide open and he enters, pushing the "10" button, the doors smoothly sliding shut. Moments later, Hank struts down the hallway to Dr. Irvine's office. He knocks and sticks his head in.

"Hello?"

Hank scans the reception area, it's vacant. Entering, he approaches the second door to the laboratory. He knocks again.

"Doc, you here?"

"Hank my boy, come on in," Mr. Gustav answers.

"Oh, I'm sorry. I thought Dr. Irvine would be here tonight?"

"Sorry, he won't be joining us tonight. This gives us a chance for you and I to discuss a business opportunity."

"What kind of business?"

"Oh, you know, the kind that consists of taking over the world." Gustav smiles as he hands Hank a white box, much like the kind one would get at a department store.

"What's this?"

"I need you to put this on," Gustav requests.

Hank opens the box with a raised eyebrow.

"Uh, what is this?"

"Just trust me, my lad."

"This is so weird," Hank responds as he reluctantly follows Gustav's request.

Later, Hank stands in front of the mirror looking at himself. All he has on are a pair of black leather pants that were four sizes too big. Hank holds the excess leather in his fist at his waist. The look on his face indicates he feels stupid standing there, holding these ridiculous pants up that Gustav insisted he put on.

"I'm sorry, man, but they don't fit," Hank hollers at Gustav who is across the laboratory at Dr. Irvine's lab table. He's fidgeting with a device.

"You'll grow into them," Gustav replies as he approaches Hank.

"What?" Hank asks with a confused look on his face.

With a cold gaze on his face, Gustav points a remote device at Hank and pushes the red button which brings Hank instantly to his knees. He grimaces in pain as he tries to move his arms to his head, but he has no control over his body. Then Gustav pushes the yellow button which causes Hank to yell in agony. Gustav watches as Hank's body begins to transform. The muscle in his arms and legs begin to swell. Hank's ears become pointed as his nose and mouth begin to form what appears to be a dog-like snout. His fingernails turn into claws and a coat of blonde hair explodes on his chest and back which creeps up to his neck and jaw line and onto his cheeks.

Hank's body falls, face first on the floor, panting heavily. Gustav pushes the red button again, which releases Hank from the device's grip. Slowly, Hank begins to move, first to his knees, then one knee, and then finally to his feet. He slowly turns his attention back to his reflection. He snorts at his appearance.

"What happened to me?" he growls.

Mr. Gustav walks behind him to where Hank could see him in the mirror.

"You've been enhanced, handpicked by me. Only you can assist us in achieving our goal."

Gustav walks around admiring his new pet. "Now, first things first, I'm in control. Everything you do will be by my command. You have been given a unique gift. You have power that is nearly unmatched by any human. The world can be yours. As long as you do as I say. Do you understand?"

"No, I don't. This isn't what I signed up for."

"But I'm willing to give you so much more!" Gustav states.

"How?"

"Trust me."

"What if I don't want to?"

Gustav simply pushes a button on his remote device which brings Hank immediately to his knees as his gasps for air.

"You no longer have a say so," Gustav says.

Hank holds his head as he rolls around on the floor, moaning.

"I'm giving you the opportunity to be one of the most powerful beings on the planet!" Gustav yells. "It just happens to be under our control." He straightens out his suit jacket and says, "Just remember, you wanted this."

Gustav watches the creature grimace for a moment then asks, "Are you ready to obey?"

"Yes, sir," Hank answers through gritted teeth.

"Very well," Gustav replies as he mans the remote control again.

Instantly, Hank is free of the torment. He breathes heavily as if he had just finished a marathon.

"Now, I don't like doing this. We are on the same team," Gustav said. "Your compliance is important to our success. Do you understand?"

Hank nods in confirmation. The snarl on his face indicates that he did not like the strings attached to this new power.

"Great!" Gustav smiles. "First on our agenda, rid ourselves of the pesky VoLt thing."

"What?" Hank asks as a look of bewilderment comes over his face. "How?"

"Like I said, you are now one of the most powerful beings on the planet. Nothing can stop you. Nothing."

Hank looks at himself again. He begins flexing his arms and chest. His eyes widen at the results he sees. His fangs slightly appear as a small grin comes to surface.

"So, are you game?" Gustav asks.

"Gladly!" Hank answers in a delighted yet angry tone.

"That's what I want to hear!"

"What's after that?" Hank asks. He turns his attention to Gustav.

"Like I said earlier, global domination," Gustav says with a raised eyebrow and a sinister grin. "Any ideas how to draw him out, Kronox?"

Hank looks a little confused after hearing the name of his new alter ego. He takes a moment to let the name sink in. Then he turns his attention from Gustav and looks back at the mirror.

"I think I have an idea."

CHAPTER 20

Ginger and Dustin enjoy a light conversation as they walk side by side. Dustin had to admit to himself that this is the happiest he had been in a long while. The doubts in his mind had him questioning everything since he first enrolled in the seminary that summer after he left college in 2002. He left college mainly due to Ginger. The realization that Ginger would never see him as anything more than a friend had him feeling lost and alone. Dustin answered the calling that had been tugging on his heart as he focused on his new life at the seminary. He knew where the voices of doubt came from, he always knew. Dustin began to realize that as long as he heard the voices of doubt, he knew he had to rely on his faith and continue his track down that path. But now, those voices were finally silent.

"You want some hot chocolate?" Dustin asks as they pass a coffee shop.

"Yeah, sounds good!" Ginger smiles.

They walk inside and buy two cups of hot chocolate. They step back out into the cool England wind sipping on the hot drinks. Ginger takes a couple of steps ahead of Dustin, then turns around and stops in front of him. Dustin's eyebrows rise as he comes to a sudden stop. They gaze into each other's eyes. Dustin's mind races to determine where this is going. Ginger leans in close to where they were nearly rubbing noses.

"That hits the spot," Dustin says softly.

"Sure does," she replies as she leans in and kisses him on the lips.

His heart races at the realization of what's going on. Her lips feel and taste the same as they did nearly six years ago. They both lean back at the same time and smile at each other. Then they turn and continue their walk down the sidewalk hand in hand, as Dustin's head spins in delight.

"My apartment is right over there," Ginger states.

"Oh, okay," Dustin says. He feels his heart start to race again. How would the evening end? Would he get another chance to kiss her, and what does this all mean? Is Hank out of the picture now? Would he finally be able to start a life with the love of his life?

They dodge the cars as they cross the street and stop in front of the steps that lead up to her apartment building. She stands there, smiling, slightly swaying back and forth. Dustin could see the battle going on in her eyes. The battle is raging in him as well. But something speaks to his heart. It's telling him to be patient just a bit longer. Dustin wants to drown out that voice, but he can't. Ginger may still be somewhat vulnerable. And he doesn't want to rush into anything now. He's waited his whole life for this chance. Dustin knows he needs to listen to that small, still voice. He decides to ease her struggle and simply reaches in and gives her a hug.

"I had a lot of fun this evening," he says.

"Me too. Are you sure you have to go and help your young friend, Cameron?" she asks.

He didn't want to. He wanted to spend the evening with her. But he had to admit, he completely forgot about Cameron. Internally, he was a little embarrassed that he did.

"Yeah, he seemed a little distraught. Poor kid," he says.

"Well, it's awful nice of you to help him out. You're a true man of character," she replies as she held onto him.

Normally, a compliment like that would mean a lot to him, but those words stung a little coming from her. It meant that he had passed on several opportunities that other guys were able to be a part of. Dustin always felt he needed to in order to keep his *character* in check.

"Well…"

Suddenly, he is interrupted by a sound that seems to be a growling noise quickly approaching them from behind, much like a charging bull. Before he could turn around, Dustin feels sharp claws dig into his shoulders as he is yanked away abruptly. Then, almost instantly, Dustin finds himself thrown onto a hood of a nearby car with a thunderous thud. Ginger is shoved to the ground from the force of the attack. Looking up, she sees a monstrous blonde creature in black leather shorts picking Dustin up by his throat.

"You pathetic little twerp!" the creature growls.

The blonde monster lifts Dustin up off the car and flings him over his shoulder. Dustin's body flies, flipping in the air, landing on his back on the concrete steps.

"Dustin!" Ginger screams as she runs over to his side.

Ginger softly touches his face, seemingly trying to assess his condition. Then she looks up only to see the golden creature approach them. Horror covers her face, fearing the monster's next move. He walks over and pushes Ginger aside. Then the creature bends down, and proceeds to grab Dustin by his throat again. Ginger lies on the cold damp steps in fear as she looks over only to see the beast glaring at her.

"Where do I find VoLt?" he barks.

His snout creased with anger.

"I, I don't know," she answers nervously.

"Well, you better find him!"

The monster stands up and lifts Dustin off the ground with relative ease. Dustin hangs there lifeless in the creature's clutch.

"Now you have something else to report on!" he says with a conceited glare aimed at Ginger.

"Please, put him down," she pleads.

"Put him down?" The creature releases an evil low chuckle. "My pleasure."

He lowers Dustin down to where they are face to face.

"You're pathetic. Always have been, always will be!"

Then he drops Dustin to the ground as the golden creature proceeds to kick him in the chest, causing Dustin to flail back as blood begins streaming out of his mouth. Dustin falls to the ground, motionless.

"Where are you, VoLt? Here I am! Your worthy opponent!" he shouts to the rooftops around him.

Ginger sits curled up at the bottom of the stairs in paralyzing fear.

"You're all pathetic!" he says, glaring back at Ginger.

Taking a couple of steps back and glancing around at the rooftops around him, he proceeds to run down the street only to vanish into the city's darkness.

"Dustin," she says as she runs to his side. She kneels down and holds him in her arms. Tears begin streaming down her face.

"Somebody, help!" she screams at the windows of her apartment building. "Help me, please!"

A shadow comes to one window and pulls back the curtain. Ginger sees the figure and shouts, "We need an ambulance! Hurry! Please!"

Turning her head back to Dustin, she sobs as she pulls Dustin close to her and gently rocks him back and forth.

CHAPTER 21

Gustav sits in the back of a black van, two blocks away from the prison that holds Professor Zen. Rechecking his watch and then glancing out the front window of the van again, he taps his fingers continuously on the armrest of his seat. He releases a heavy breath of anxiety as it appears he is trying to determine where his new pet could be. Suddenly the back van doors fling open as the blonde creature stands there, both doors held open with his freakishly monstrous arms.

Gustav releases a sigh, this time in relief. He coldly looks at his new pet.

"Any luck?" Gustav asks.

"No, he didn't show up, but I did take care of some personal business."

"Very well."

Gustav slightly rolls his eyes, as if trying to determine the personal business the kronog dealt with and wondering if it would be something he would have to deal with himself shortly.

"Let's do this!" the gold monster says in a pregame motivation manner.

The front doors of the police station open. Mr. Gustav and Hank, disguised in a black wig and cheesy moustache, enters along with their driver and another associate that Hank hadn't seen prior to tonight. The officer behind the counter looks over the foursome and stands up.

"Can I help you?" the officer asks in a flat, guarded tone.

"Yes, I'm here to see Professor Zen," Gustav states coldly.

"Sorry, visiting hours are over," the guard answers in robotic-like demeanor.

"We're not here to visit."

The officer didn't respond, but begins to pick up the phone for possible assistance. Gustav smoothly pulls out the remote device from his inside suit pocket as the guard watches his every move. A sense of urgency comes over the guard's face at the realization of the dire predicament in which he quickly finds himself.

"The more, the messier," Gustav warns.

Then he pushes the switch changing Hank and the other two associates into the kronogs.

"I need help up here!" the officer yells into the phone as he pulls the gun from the holster. One of the kronogs leaps in the air and tackles the policeman.

Hank, now in Kronox form, runs alongside Gustav and the other kronog as they head down the hallway past the guard's post. The golden beast takes the lead, breaking through doors on their way to the cell where Zen is being held. Reaching a secured gate, the newly teamed up kronog pulls out a badge and swipes the security panel as the barred door pops open. Hank looks at Gustav with an impressed look as he realizes they had recruited a cop somewhere along the way. Finally, yet quickly, they approach Zen's cell where they find him standing, waiting, and ready to leave.

"Zen, party of one?" the Kronox says smugly.

"Here," Zen replies.

The kronog swipes the card again, allowing Zen's doors to unlock. Zen steps out and quickly admires the new Kronox.

"Shall we go?" the professor asks.

"Right this way," the kronog answers.

Rapid gunfire fills the station as the other two kronogs return fire with the rifles that they acquired on their way out. The agility and accuracy that the kronogs possess sent the police retreating upstairs and down hallways. The kronogs appeared to be able to shoot from any and all angles. The five escape out the front door and leap into the van and speed off as some of the officers chase after them, opening fire on the black van as sirens sound off from the station.

The bells of Berthel Church chime, piercing the night sky as it echoes over the neighborhood. Cameron sits in the second pew, patiently waiting for Dustin to arrive. Reluctantly, he seems to be counting the obvious number of chimes.

"Seven, eight, nine…" he says softly yet sternly. "Oh for crying out loud, Dustin. Where are you?"

Cameron turns around hoping that he magically would see Dustin come up from behind him. Nobody is there. Nobody is here for him, nobody.

His nostrils flare at the realization that Dustin had stood him up. He turns back around and rests his arms on the back of the pew in front of him. He looks up at the cross that hangs in front of the sanctuary just behind the pulpit.

"I thought I could trust him. I thought I could depend on him."

He stares off as his fingers fidget on the pew, possibly pondering the fate of his friend, Jayden.

"I'm going to lose her. Lose her to them!"

Cameron quickly jumps to his feet with frustration in his eyes. His jaw flinches as he smashes his teeth firmly together. Glaring back at the cross, he steps out of the pew and storms out of the church.

CHAPTER 22

Ginger sits beside the bed where Dustin lies unconscious. The monitor beeps in unison with his heartbeat. She gazes up at the clock, 2:07 a.m., as she continues to hold his motionless hand. Ginger looks on at him through tired, makeup-smudged eyes. Hearing a soft knock at the door, she only briefly takes her eyes off of him and glances at the door. The door of the hospital room opens as Pastor Phillips enters with a grave look on his face.

"Pastor Phillips, thank you for coming! I didn't know who else to call."

The pastor, dressed in a navy hooded sweatshirt and gray sweatpants, appears to be at a loss for words as he gazes upon his battered associate. Finally, without looking at Ginger, he asks, "What happened?"

"We were just telling each other good night when this monster came out of nowhere," Ginger says, retelling the event. "He attacked Dustin relentlessly, and then asked me where he could find the creature, VoLt."

She pauses, seemingly struggling with the reasoning behind the attack.

"I think he was trying to use me as bait to lure out VoLt."

Phillips looks at Ginger with a scared, confused look. "I don't know what to do," she cries.

"Neither do I."

The pastor steps out of the hospital room after sitting quietly for hours with Ginger at Dustin's side. He walks down the hallway toward the floor's lobby. He stops in front of the coffee vending machine and fiddles for change in his pocket. Pulling out a couple of coins he drops them in the slot and selects black coffee. Bending slightly, he grabs the cup and begins sipping it. The pastor gazes out the floor's lobby window at the slow rising sun. The soft noise from the television fills the empty room. Phillips breathes heavily as he seems to be trying to grasp Dustin's condition and situation. Slowly, he begins to realize that it is the BBC's morning news show running on the lobby's television. Almost cautiously, he turns and focuses his attention on the news reports. A seemingly unbelievable story is running as the pastor stands motionless as the news begins to sink in.

"We have numerous reports throughout the area of monstrous creatures terrorizing the city of London. We cannot confirm or deny that one of these creatures is the same creature known as VoLt that our own Ginger Nevine has been reporting on over the past week. We are still attempting to gather information as we speak," the newsman reports.

"We are getting new information regarding the attack at Scotland Yard. We can now confirm that

Professor Lucas Zen has escaped. Lucas Zen had been convicted of murder of two individuals in the massive explosion in the old river business district. Leads to the newsroom indicate that Zen's escape was with the aid of the same dog-like creatures that he was seen with just days before the deadly explosion nearly two years ago. Professor Zen himself referred to these creatures as 'kronogs.'"

Pastor Phillips's face turns pale as he quickly sits in a chair in the lobby. Placing the coffee down, he clasps his hands together and prays, "Dear Lord, be with our city as we face these demons. And place your healing hand on Dustin, who may be our only hope, whom you have sent to protect us."

Just before nine in the morning, the doctor came in with the results of Dustin's condition. Phillips stood behind Ginger holding her shoulders for support.

"Dustin is suffering from a concussion, bruised kidneys, and a punctured lung from cracked ribs. If he received this beating from the same creature that they are reporting on the news, I would have to say he's very fortunate," the doctor said. "All we can do is hope he wakes up soon."

Phillips and Ginger are silent as the doctor's report sinks in.

"We'll continue to monitor him, but it is going to be day to day for a while."

Phillips shakes his head slightly, indicating they didn't have time to sit and wait.

"Thank you, Doctor?" Phillips said hinting for a name.

"Dr. Sherman," he answers.

"Okay, thank you, Dr. Sherman."

Ginger just nods in agreement with the pastor without taking her eyes off Dustin. The doctor excuses himself as the pastor walks over to the room's window.

"Ginger, I need to go for a while. But I'll be right back."

He turns around and looks at Ginger. "Our church secretary should be contacting his family. Do you know them?"

She nods yes. Ginger's wide eyes seem to notice the lack of color in the pastor's complexion.

"Are you okay, sir?"

"Uh, just a little concerned," he pauses. "I'll be back soon," he says as he leaves the room.

CHAPTER 23

The door to Dustin's quarters opens as Pastor Phillips enters. Closing the door and locking it, he looks around the room. The pastor focuses his attention on the dresser. Gripping the dresser and smashing his teeth together in hopes of acquiring extra strength, he pulls the dresser back revealing the hidden door. Opening the small panel, he finds Dustin's black cloak and the medallion hanging on a hook in the tunnel's entrance. The pastor lifts the items off the hook and places them on Dustin's bed. He proceeds to close the small door and pushes the dresser back in place. Looking around the room, the pastor finds Dustin's backpack that he carries the cloak and medallion in. Shoving them in the bag, he quickly leaves the room.

Moments later, Phillips knocks on Sharon's office door.

"Come in," she answers.

"Did you get a hold of Dustin's family?"

"No, the number we have is invalid, according to the phone system. I don't know what to do."

"Well, we'll try again here in a while," he responds soberly.

"Are you okay, Reverend?" Sharon asks.

"Oh, I'll just be glad when Dustin's out of the woods."

"You really care about that boy, don't you?"

"Yeah," he answers, quickly holding his breath, seemingly trying to keep the tear from falling that suddenly formed in his eye.

Just then, something caught Sharon's attention, behind Pastor Phillips. She turns her head slightly to address the person approaching them.

"Well hello, Arnie. How are you?" she asks.

"Just fine, and you?" the echoed voice responds as he approaches the secretary's door.

The pastor turns around to greet his old friend. Phillips extends his arm out and shakes the detective's hand. They haven't really spoken to each other in over a year. Not since Arnie helped out with getting Jessica Parsons a new identity and getting her safely out of the country after she escaped Professor Zen's fusion regenerator and the devastating explosion in the old business district. The same explosion that took Tim Warner's life.

"Good morning, Arn."

"Good morning, Pastor. Did I catch you at a bad time?"

Phillips's eyes pop open wide in response to the seemingly loaded question by Detective Hobbs.

"Uh, no," he answers, even though his eyes and facial expression indicated that he's trying to believe his own words that this wasn't a bad time.

"Let's go to my office," Phillips suggests, aiming his arm down the hallway.

"Good to see you, Sharon," Hobbs says to the secretary as they step away.

"Good to see you too, Arnie."

As they made their way into the pastor's office, Hobbs tries to ease the tension in the conversation.

"Sorry to pop in on you like this."

"You're fine, Arnie. What can I do for you?"

"Well, unfortunately, I'm here on business."

Arnie motions toward the chair, gesturing if he could sit down.

"Yes, please do," the pastor replies as he proceeds to sit in his own chair.

"Well, like I said, I'm more or less here on business, but I would like for this conversation to be off the record. What is said here stays between you and me. Is that okay?"

"Absolutely," the pastor replies as a bead of sweat begins to form on his temple. It was standard protocol for counseling to be confidential, but with a member of the police force coming to meet with him, he didn't know what the intentions might exactly be.

"Great, thanks," the detective pauses for a moment, then he begins. "We've been friends for a long time. Ever since we were ten or so. So, we know each other pretty well, right, Jack?"

Calling him by his first name seemingly made this more of a personal matter.

"Sure, Arnie. What's wrong?"

"Well, about two years ago, as you recall, we did that favor for Jessica Parsons, changing her name to Jessie Warner and relocating her to the US."

"Right," Jack replies.

"Well, later, I did some checking. The only Jessica Parsons I could find was an elderly woman that was a member of this church. The same woman we had a funeral for just within days of each other. I've been trying to wrap my head around that, but I can't. Then, I read the report that had the VoLt creature at the scene of the explosion where supposedly Miss Parsons and Mr. Warner were killed and where Zen and his associates were apprehended."

Jack sits quietly as he continues to listen to Arnie cover the facts. Hearing each account of the events causes his eyes to widen. He shakes his head subtly, as if it still seemed unbelievable to him as well, as if this is the first time he heard it.

"And there's also the rumors of VoLt coming to the aid of that young man in our church, Cameron, I think is his name."

Hobbs looks at Jack for confirmation on the accuracy of the reports. Jack sits still with his face now void of any emotion.

Hobbs continues, "Then only to have VoLt show up at a party where Abbey, our head deacon's daughter, was assaulted. So, I'm trying to make the connection between Ms. Parsons, VoLt, and the kids in our church. I mean, since you and our youth minister are the ones that called me down to help her, I was hoping at some point you would be able to shed some light on this subject for me." Arnie shifts his weight a little in his chair in an attempt to get comfortable in an uneasy situation.

"Then I hear about some creature nearly beating the life out of this man. I go to investigate and I discover that it's none other than our own youth minister that was attacked." Arnie paused. "Is it just me, or does Dustin seem closely connected to where the trouble is?"

Pastor Phillips gives his old friend a stressed smile as a couple more beads of sweat formed on his forehead.

Later that afternoon, the pastor returns to Dustin's hospital room. Ginger holds his hand as Dustin continues to remain unconscious. The pastor carries the black backpack containing the medallion over his shoulder. He looks over Ginger and notices the weariness in her eyes.

"Ginger, you look tired. Why don't you go and get some rest? I'll stay here and I'll call you if anything changes," Phillips said.

"Oh, I'm fine, really, I'm fine."

"I insist. One of us needs to recharge. You've been here since last night. Rest up and come back and you can relieve me."

Ginger looks at Dustin as she continues to caress his hand.

"Did you get a hold of the family?"

"No, not yet, but we're trying."

Trying not to be pushy, he walks over to the other side of Dustin's bed and pleads his request. "Ginger, please."

She lets out a sigh as she squeezes his hand one more time, hoping it would somehow cause him to wake up.

"Okay," she answers in a deflated tone, "but call me if anything changes."

"Will do."

Reverend Phillips walks over and gently rubs her shoulders in an attempt to help her release Dustin. Ginger slowly stands up and gives a small smile of appreciation to the pastor. She walks over to the door and turns around to give Dustin one more look then she opens the door and slowly walks out.

"Lord, forgive me for that impending lie," the reverend said. He took off the backpack and looks at the sleeping Dustin. "I thought she would never leave."

Phillips opens the backpack and pulls out the medallion. He walks over to the door and looks out the small ten inch by ten inch square window. He can see two nurses at the floor's desk. They were busy charting and answering the phones. Slowly and gently, the pastor locks the door. Then he walks over to Dustin and pries open his hand. Holding the medallion by the leather straps, he lowers the medallion to where it just barely touch Dustin's palm.

Dustin's hand flinches instantly, grabbing the gold pendant. The pastor witnesses the transformation begin to take place instantly as he looks up and sees Dustin arch his back and pop his eyes open.

He looks over at Phillips with a look of pain and shock. The pastor quickly tries to pry the medallion out of Dustin's grasp, but his rapid increasing strength makes it impossible for him.

"Dustin, you have to let it go!" the reverend says with his face flushing red as sweat begins to form on his forehead while he tries desperately to take back the medallion.

Dustin growls in agony as he opens his palm allowing the pastor to take back the gold V pendant. Dustin quickly transforms back to himself again as Phillips breathes heavily in time with Dustin.

"What…what was that?" Dustin asks as he still grimaces in pain looking at Reverend Phillips.

"It sounded like a good idea in my head at the time. I guess I should have thought it out more."

Dustin lightly gasps as he begins to feel his injures from his attacker while he tosses back and forth slightly in his bed. The pastor places the medallion back in the backpack and lets out a sigh of relief as he zips it up.

"Where am I?" Dustin moans.

"At the hospital."

A sudden shock came over Dustin. "Where's Ginger?"

"She's fine. She's been at your side all night. She left just before I pulled this stunt."

Taking a few moments, allowing Dustin to catch his breath, the pastor is eager to ask the next question.

"Do you know what did this to you?"

"Uh…no. All I know is that it was big, mean, and strong. And it didn't like me," Dustin answers.

Dustin lies still as he tries to recall the events from the previous night.

"He called me a little twerp."

He tries to shift his weight around a little to find some comfort. Dustin continues with his recollection. "Funny, that was the second person to call me a twerp in the past two days."

"Who else called you that?" the pastor asks, as if starting to make the quick connection.

Dustin turns his head to look directly at Phillips. A stunned stare came over him.

"Hank."

"Hank? Hank Jamerson?" Phillips asks back.

Grimacing in pain, Dustin tries his best to sit up in his bed.

"Yeah," Dustin replies as he sits still for a moment at the realization of Hank's newfound abilities. "Are you kidding me? Of all people," Dustin says as he closes his eyes, cringing in pain and slightly arching his back in discomfort. The pain from his injury and the excess of knowledge momentarily overwhelmed his brain.

"How could he have obtained the powers to be a kronog? A really, really strong kronog at that?" the pastor asks.

"I don't know," Dustin pauses. "I guess it would make sense. No wonder he was so angry."

"So, it's not that he knew you are VoLt, but it's because you were with Ginger," Phillips says.

"And he was after Ginger to get to VoLt, I just happened to be in the wrong place at the wrong time," Dustin concludes.

"How could this have happened?" the pastor asks.

Dustin sits perplexed for a moment.

"Well, I did see him meet with Gustav a couple of nights ago." Then he turns to look at the pastor, "I guess they are picking up where Zen left off."

Dustin notices Phillips's face instantly turn pale.

"Sir, what's wrong?"

The pastor remains quiet for a moment, as if he doesn't want to inform Dustin of the latest news.

"First, call me Jack, for crying out loud. I think we're close enough now to be on first name basis with each other."

Then the pastor's face turned grim.

"Zen escaped from jail last night. And I believe it was by the same thing that did this to you that aided him in his escape."

"What? Oh for crying out loud!"

Dustin looks at Phillips with an exhausted look, "What kind of test am I going through now?"

"I wish I knew," Phillips answers.

CHAPTER 24

Zen stands in front of the glass wall of the London Science Research building in Dr. Irvine's laboratory, overlooking the city of London. Dressed in his tan Italian suit, he sips on his gourmet coffee.

"This is indeed one of the finest facilities I've been in, and the fact that it's right under the government's nose makes it all that sweeter," Zen says.

"Uh, why, uh, thank you Professor Zen," Dr. Irvine stammers through the compliment. "I just want to, uh, say, uh, what an honor it is to finally meet you."

Mr. Gustav stands in the distance watching the interaction between Zen and Irvine. The doctor is a flight risk. Gustav already had to track him down late last night as he found Irvine attempting to leave for France. Despite the fact that Irvine is on staff at the LSRC, it is Gustav's group that had been funding the top secret experiments regarding Hascetemic, which is the human and animal steroid correlation with the electronic triggering to mutating capabilities.

Gustav couldn't let his most valuable doctor take an unscheduled vacation just as he recovered the most brilliant scientist from prison. The two of them could make a lot of waves in the science field. Gustav had everything invested, including his own life. He managed to convince his worthiness to his superiors in the remote mountains of Pakistan, but he was warned that if he didn't produce valid results, that it would literally be his own head.

A refrigerator door slams shut next to the kitchenette section of the lab. Jamerson twists off the cap of a power shake and begins drinking it as he approaches Gustav.

"So, what's next?" Hank asks as he wipes his mouth with his sleeve after gulping the power shake that he routinely drinks every day.

Gustav looks at him with a slight hint of disgust at the realization that their success rests on the shoulders of this Neanderthal.

"Go back home. Go back to your routine. Don't change anything. If you have practice, go to practice. If you have a television interview, go to the interview. You have a girlfriend, go—"

"Had a girlfriend," Hank replies.

"What do you mean, 'had a girlfriend'?" Gustav asks back in an agitated tone.

"Yeah, we kinda broke up—"

"Well, fix it! She's our best hope of locating VoLt. She's the only one that has been close to him, except for Jessica Parsons," Gustav barks.

"Jessica Parsons?"

"Forget her, she's yesterday's news. Focus! Patch things with your girl. Can you do that?"

"Hey, I'm Hank 'The Tank' Jamerson. No problem," Hank says as he slaps Gustav on the shoulder.

"Great," Gustav says as he catches his balance from being thrust forward from the friendly gesture.

"Later, dudes!" Hank yells at Professor Zen and Dr. Irvine as he waves at them, exiting the laboratory.

Zen looks at Gustav with a questionable glance regarding his handpicked selection to be the Kronox.

"It'll be fine," Gustav says, trying to convince himself. Straightening his posture and smoothing out his suit, he walks over to the window and tries to reassure himself again. "It'll be fine."

CHAPTER 25

Ginger rolls over in her bed and looks at the clock, two thirty in the afternoon. She rubs her swollen eyes. Taking all the energy she has, she sits up in bed. She sits there silently, pondering what she should do next. She reaches for her cell phone, possibly to call the hospital to check on Dustin's condition. She flips it open only to see a blank screen. She attempts to power it up, but it doesn't respond.

"Great, I forgot to charge it up," she says in a disappointed tone.

She begins to look for her charger when she hears a knock on the door. She freezes, wondering if she really did hear the knock. Then the door knocks again with a heavy fist. Jumping to her feet, she dashes to the door with panic on her face, seemingly preparing herself for the worst. As she opens the door, her look of concern turns to a look of confusion.

"Hank?"

"Hey, babe," Hank responds.

"What are you doing here?"

"I came to see you."

"Why?" she asks as the level of frustration became apparent in her eyes.

"Please hear me out, babe," he says, almost pleading for her to let him in. "I was wrong. I shouldn't have treated you that way. And I'm sorry that I treated little Dustin that way. I just want to make it up to you."

"Did you hear about Dustin?" she asks.

"No, what?"

Ginger turns around leaving the door open. Hank takes it as a sign that he can come in. He follows Ginger as she goes into the bathroom to grab some tissues.

"Babe, what happened to him?" he asks with a slight gleam in his eyes that she didn't see.

"Some kind of monster attacked us and nearly ripped him apart," she answers as the tears began to well up in her eyes again.

"Was it that VoLt creep?"

"No, it wasn't VoLt. They say VoLt is not mean like that."

"Was it stronger than VoLt?" Hank asks as he walks around the room, eager to hear her response.

"I don't know. All I know is that it seemed to be filled with hate. Hate that he took out on Dustin."

"What did he want?"

"I think it wanted me to tell him where he can find VoLt."

"Do you know where VoLt is?" Hank asks.

"No."

"Are you sure?"

"Yes," she answers as she slightly glares at Hank.

"Well, next time you see VoLt, tell him someone's looking for him."

Ginger looks at Hank with annoyance.

"Whatever. Anyway, why are you here?" she asks.

"Us! That's why I'm here," Hank replies.

"Oh, Hank. I just don't know." She rubs her forehead with her right arm while she rests her left hand on her hip. "I mean, there's a lot going on."

The blank look on Hank's face indicated that he wasn't getting the hint from Ginger. Slightly shaking her head, she says, "I need to get back to the hospital and check on Dustin."

"What, do you love him?" Hank asks as a scowl came over his face.

"What? It's Dustin, we've been friends forever. You know that," Ginger says.

"Yeah, but he always wanted it to be more," Hank responds.

"I don't know about that, besides, I was never in that place to be more than friends—"

"And now—" Hank interrupts.

"And now, there's a lot going on. I need to go, Hank. I have to check on him."

"Okay, let me take you," Hank offers.

"You're kidding."

"No, I'm serious," Hank says, trying to put on a sincere look.

Ginger pauses for a second as she looks at him, possibly trying to determine his true sincerity.

"Really?" she asks.

"Really. See, I'm trying," Hank says as he motions toward the door.

Ginger follows him with arms crossed and raised eyebrows.

CHAPTER 26

The brunette nurse finishes taking Dustin's blood pressure. Her gentle touch brings some calmness over him. Making note of the numbers, she looks over Dustin.

"I don't understand. You were completely out just a mere couple of hours ago, and now you're almost good to go home," the nurse says with a smile regarding Dustin's condition.

"Almost," both Dustin and Phillips said at the same time.

"Yes, I need the doctor to check you over one more time. Besides, you did suffer a concussion and some broken ribs. We just want to make sure you're well enough to go home like you insist." She pauses as she looks skeptically at Dustin. "If the doctor agrees, then he'll sign your release."

"Oh, okay," Dustin softly replies as he begins to feel some concern about the doctor's examination of him.

"I'll have him paged. It shouldn't be too long of a wait," the attractive nurse says as she places her hand on his shoulder in a caring gesture.

"Oh, okay," he replies.

"Thank you, ma'am," the pastor says.

They remain quiet until the door closes behind her after she exits the room.

"I think it would be in our best interest if you were released before the authorities came in to ask you about the creature that did this to you."

"Yeah, I have to warn Ginger, somehow," Dustin replies as he almost entertains the thought of finally ending any chance of Hank pushing his way back into their lives.

"You might want to carefully plan your next move regarding that," Phillips says as he guesses the thought that ran through Dustin's mind.

Dustin sits up in his bed as the doctor presses the cold stethoscope against his back.

"Okay, take a deep breath," the doctor orders as Dustin responds. "And release."

Dustin exhales as the doctor continues to listen to his lungs. Pulling out the stethoscope from his ears, he looks at Dustin with skepticism. He shakes his head side to side in a gesture that indicated he didn't quite understand the sudden change in Dustin's condition.

He stands in front of Dustin, almost pondering whether to release him or not. Then he pulls out the chrome plated pin light and checks Dustin's eyes again. Dustin silently prays that his pupils respond as they should as the light flashes in each eye.

"I don't think I recall such a quick recovery from a concussion like this."

"Uh, thanks I guess," Dustin answers innocently.

"Okay, I guess you are good to go," Doctor Sherman says. "I would take it easy for a while. Your lung and ribs were injured, and still may be susceptible to being re-injured. I wish I could explain the quick turnaround, but," Sherman pauses as he looks over at Pastor Phillips, "I guess that's the power of prayer, right?"

"Uh, right," Phillips responds with a smile.

The doctor again shakes his head and signs the release papers.

"So I can go?" Dustin asks.

"Yes, you are free to go."

"Great!" Dustin replies as he quickly stands up from the bed.

The doctor, a little surprised at Dustin's rapid amount of energy, reiterates his instructions. "I'm serious, take it easy for a while."

"Yes, sir," both Dustin and Phillips respond.

The doctor shakes his head again and excuses himself as he leaves the room.

Dustin turns to look at Pastor Phillips and smiles, "I wonder if running through subways and sewers and fighting bad guys would constitute 'taking it easy'?"

The doors of the elevator open and Hank and Ginger step out. As they approach the nurses' station, the brunette nurse looks up at Ginger and smiles.

"He's awake now."

"He is?" Ginger responds.

The nurse's eyes pop open wide when she realizes that Hank Jamerson is standing in front of her.

"Tank Jamerson! Wow, it's a thrill to meet you!" she says as she stands up to shake his hand. "Would you mind signing an autograph for my son?"

"Nope, not at all," Hank responds with a hint of annoyance from either the never-ending recognition he continuously receives or the fact that Dustin seemed to be recovering.

The nurse pulls out a piece of paper and pen for Hank. He proceeds to sign another autograph, as Ginger walks over to Dustin's room.

"His name is Jonathan. He is such a big fan!"

"That's great," Hank said.

As Hank scribbles on the paper, Ginger quickly comes back to the desk.

"He's not there!" Ginger states.

"Oh, I'm sorry," the nurse responded, "I didn't finish." Realizing that her excitement of meeting Hank "The Tank" Jamerson interrupted her train of thought. "They just released him about thirty minutes ago."

"Released him?" Ginger questions, trying to understand the sudden improvement of Dustin's condition. "How can this be? Just hours ago, he was unconscious. Now he's going home?"

"I know, it has us baffled as well," the nurse responds, trying to gain as much eye contact with Hank as possible.

"Weird," Hank responds with almost a detection of annoyance over Dustin's sudden recovery.

"Who did he leave with?" Ginger asks as her mood begins to change.

"I believe his pastor took him home," the brunette answers.

"Really?" Ginger responds sarcastically, "I'm glad he kept me informed."

"Great. Let's find him," Hank responds as he tries to break away from the nurse's star-struck stare.

CHAPTER 27

Pastor Phillips escorts Dustin back to his living quarters. Dustin seems to be moving fine on his own, but the pastor wants to be there just in case. Releasing a sigh of relief, he glances over the room. He wants to just flop down in his bed and rest, but he knows he can't, duty calls. Dustin turns his attention to his dresser, but more importantly, he focuses his attention on what hid behind it.

"I guess I better get to work."

"Are you up for this?" Phillips asks.

"I guess I have to be," Dustin replies as he pushes the dresser back, feeling pain shoot up and down his right side. "I'm sure Ginger will come calling soon."

"I'll cover for you," Pastor Phillips replies.

Dustin has to fight the sudden urge to laugh at the pastor's ability to bend the truth, or the lack of successfully being able to.

"Are you sure?" Dustin asks as he gives the pastor a crooked smile.

"Well, I'll give my best."

Pastor Phillips walks out into the congregation and proceeds to head to his office when the church's front door opens. At first, all he could see were silhouettes of two individuals, a man and a woman. He nods to the couple in a manner letting them know they were welcome to come in. He continues toward his office when suddenly the woman speaks up.

"Pastor Phillips, is Dustin here?" shouts the female figure.

Phillips freezes and turns around to see the couple quickly approach him down the center aisle.

"Ginger?" he asks.

"Is Dustin here?"

"I'm sorry dear, but no," Phillips says coolly.

"He's not in his room?" she asks.

"No, I'm sorry. He said he had some business of an urgent matter that he needed to tend to," the pastor replies, carefully choosing his words. "I apologize, Ginger. I was just on my way to notify you that Dustin was released."

"I just don't understand the sudden change in his condition."

"It does appear to be rather miraculous," the pastor replies, carrying an unbelievable look on his face.

"Well, what kind of 'urgent business' did he need to tend to?"

"Oh, I'm not allowed to say, my dear…"

Ginger didn't seem to be hearing Phillips answer her question. Instead, her eyes shifts widely back and forth as if she was attempting to figure out where he could have gone so urgently.

"Was it to see that boy in his class?" she asks.

Her eyes are wide open, as if solving a mystery, almost elated with her own investigative reporting.

"Uh, I'm not too sure," the pastor replies, his brows crossing together. "Could be."

"Right," Ginger answers with a hint of frustration of the pastor's vagueness of Dustin's location.

The pastor looks at Hank as the six foot four man stands with his arms folded.

"I'm sorry, you are?" the pastor asks.

"Hank Jamerson," Hank replies with a small frown as his keeps his posture.

The pastor extends his hand out to shake as Hank slowly reaches out with his own.

"It's nice to meet you. Are you a friend of Dustin's too?"

"Uh, we used to be roommates in college."

"Oh, I see," the pastor says as he begins to show his confident side of his established role, deliberately acting as if he truly didn't know the famous soccer player that stood before him, let alone the beast that nearly ripped his associate apart.

"Is there anything I can do?" Phillips asks.

"Can you let me know if you hear from him?" she responds skeptically, in a tone that seems to be questioning the information she received from the nurse and the coy demeanor of the pastor.

"Yes, I'll wait and pray that we hear from him soon."

"Thank you," Ginger says as she puts her hand on Hank's arm in a gesture that they need to be going.

"It was nice to meet you, young man," Phillips says to Hank.

"Likewise," Hank replies.

The pastor walks around to the first two pews and begins straightening out hymnals until the two exited out the front doors. As soon as he heard the doors shut, he plops down in the pew and releases a heavy sigh.

"Dear Lord, forgive me."

He sat there for a few moments as he quietly meditated in prayer, waiting and listening for God to speak to his heart.

As Ginger and Hank walk down the steps of the church, Hank asks, "So, where to now?"

"I don't know," she answers in a frustrated tone. "I wish I could remember the name of that boy from his class."

She stops momentarily, turning around and looking back at the church.

"Just go ask him if he knows the kid's name or not," Hank states.

Ginger looks at Hank with a bit of skepticism.

"I'm surprised you want to find him too," she says.

"Hey, I'm kinda concerned about the little twerp too."

She gives Hank a small agitated glare. Ginger ponders her next move, biting her lip, hands fidgeting.

"No. I'll leave him alone. If the pastor truly knew where Dustin is, he would have told me."

She turns around and proceeds back down the sidewalk with a slight confused look on her face. Hank glances back at the church with a questionable glare.

"I wonder where the little twerp could be?" he asks under his breath.

Hearing the mumbled question, Ginger responds, "Really, Hank?"

Shaking her head in aggravation with him, Ginger said, "Let's just leave Dustin alone too. He'll turn up when he's ready to see me."

CHAPTER 28

VoLt crawls out onto the ledge of the subway corridor just as the train approaches. Crouching down, he readies himself to leap, still very much aware of the tenderness that surrounds his ribs. Taking a deep breath, he springs from all fours and lands on top of the rail car. VoLt quickly feels the sharp pain on the right side as he desperately tries to grab hold of the train. He feels the stress that his cracked ribs are under. His nails make a slight screech against the metal that causes all the hair on his back to stand up.

He growls as he tries to stretch his body out so that his frame won't hit any low clearance pipes, wires, or ceilings.

He rides the car for ninety seconds and then pushes himself off and rolls in the air, landing on all fours. Pain shoots all around his body like an electric shock. It wasn't the softest landing, but after catching his breath, he is able to do a quick assessment of his condition.

"Whew…" he says, realizing he didn't re-injure himself. "Not too bad considering," VoLt says of his current limitations.

He held his side as he attempts to straighten himself as much as his monstrous physique would allow. Looking around in the nearly pitch dark tunnel, he estimates that the LRSC should be about one mile to the north of his current location. Moving down the corridor, he locates the sewer tunnel, simply by its stench alone. He takes a couple of moments to gather his internal strength before entering the horrid smelling conditions of the passageway.

Bending down, he pulls the grate up to the sewer and lays it to the side. VoLt recalls the notes in his head regarding the sewer system mapping. Dustin previously searched the city archives of the sewer department blueprints. Despite the fact that most of the blueprints had faded considerably, it still gave him enough information to map out his own underground road map.

Slowly crouching down, he crawls into the sewer drain, quickly finding the ledge to walk along.

"Ugh," VoLt utters as he tries to power through the stench. Looking ahead, he could tell that it would be a straight shot to the research center.

Professor Zen stands at the window in the spotless laboratory, overlooking the city, a cold, blank stare on his face, his arms folded. Mr. Gustav and Dr. Irvine notice Zen's frozen posture and appear to be concerned about his mental stability. Slowly and cautiously, Gustav approaches their silent leader.

"Professor Zen, is everything okay?" Gustav asks.

"I don't know," Zen answers without turning his head to acknowledge Gustav's presence. "I've been cooped up for over a year, without the ability to conduct any research, not even as much as a post-it note to scribble down an idea."

Zen breaks from his cemented stance to turn his head in Gustav's direction.

"I left you in charge to rebuild what I used to have. Granted, you have succeeded my expectations in many areas, but I can't help but question your selection for the Kronox experiment."

Gustav exhales loudly through his nostrils in reaction to the ongoing ridicule of his handpicked selection.

"According to the plan, we needed someone that was desperate to enhance himself. Someone that was already physically fit, but had that hunger for more. He practically begged for it."

"But a sports star?" Zen questions with a noticeable scowl on his face.

"Think about it, sir. He's perfect. If we go to my superior with this widely known athletic star, and show him what we can do with him, then surely we can put any price on it."

"I realize that. He just appears to be a loose cannon."

"A loose tank," Gustav answers with a small smile, laughing at his own joke.

"Precisely," Zen answers as he turns back around to look over the city, un-amused by Gustav's humor.

The sun had all but set as the city begins to get darker and darker with each passing moment. VoLt peers around from the dumpster that sits across the loading docks of the LSRC. The alley where VoLt found himself in was considerably cleaner than most of the alleys that he had become accustomed to. Gazing up at the impressive fifteen-story structure, his gut tells him that Zen has to be close.

A dark green delivery truck starts to make its way down the roadway between the buildings. It begins to slow down as it approaches the delivery docks. It stops just as it passes the loading bay, then the reverse lights come on at the back of the truck. Short beeps start to sound as the truck proceeds to back into the docks.

Quickly, VoLt jumps up, runs around the dumpster, and leaps up with all his might, landing on top of the delivery truck with a noticeable thud. The vehicle comes to an abrupt stop with the driver jumping out. Running from the right side to the left side, the driver checks around the truck to see what had caused the loud thud. Scratching his head and letting out a sigh of relief, the delivery man gets back into the cab and proceeds to back up to the dock.

The gray-headed security guard in his gray and black uniform steps from the docking booth to check the credentials and validity of the delivery.

"What happened out there?" the guard asks.

"I don't know," answers the twenty-year man in a green, zipped jumpsuit. "Scared the bloody crud out of me though."

The delivery man climbs the stairs to the dock and reaches down to unlock the truck door. "I didn't see anything that I could have hit, but I have a feeling though what it was," he says as he turns the handle and pulls up on the rolling door of the delivery truck.

"Yep, that's what I was afraid of," says the delivery man looking over the packages in the bed of the covered truck. "That stupid kayak!"

He proceeds to shove it back in place.

"Who would want a kayak around here?" the guard asks.

"Who knows…"

As the two men look over the contents of the truck, VoLt manages to reach the overhead pipes that run along the ceiling of the docking bay. Holding on with both feet and hands, he crawls the length of the bay until he is nearly forty feet away from the two gentlemen. Looking around, he sees two swinging doors that lead inside. Taking advantage of the distraction, VoLt drops down and runs through the dock doors.

The area is dark. Most of the staff had gone home two hours earlier. Surveying the layout, he locates the service elevator. As he plans his next move, he hears a familiar voice coming in from the docking bay. The swinging doors fly open as Hank struts his way in.

"Yeah, yeah, yeah, old man," Hank says, gesturing to the senior security guard still helping out with the delivery. "I've only been coming in here every night for the past week. You think he would remember me by now," he continues in an agitated tone.

VoLt stands silently in the corner, covered by the darkness. He watches Hank stroll through the dock office and out into the sparsely lit hallway. Cautiously moving, VoLt watches Hank press the delivery elevator button.

"Come on, come on. I don't have all day," Hank mumbles to himself.

After a few seconds, the elevator arrives with a "ding." The doors slide open and Hank steps inside. Then the doors close as the light display above the elevator entrance begins to indicate the movement of the lift.

VoLt dashes over and slides to a stop in front of the elevator door. Reading the digital display, the lift stops on the tenth floor. Looking around his surroundings, he finds a staircase.

"Ten floors, that shouldn't be too bad," VoLt says to himself as he mentally prepares himself for the climb, all the while rubbing his right side.

CHAPTER 29

Doctor Irvine nervously fastens the chest shield over Hank's newly altered physique as the Kronox.

"Uh, there, uh, how does it fit?" the doctor asks.

"It's a little snug," grumbles the Kronox, looking over at Professor Zen and Mr. Gustav as the doctor securely tightens the chest plate. "Why do I have to wear this?" Kronox asks as he opens his arms, referring to the new armor.

"It's meant to protect our investment," Zen answers coldly, arms folded.

"I don't know why, I'm virtually unstoppable without it."

"If you are going to be a tank, then you might as well be suited like one," Gustav adds as he walks back and forth with controlled anticipation.

"So, what's the game plan?" the Kronox asks as he looks at his reflection in the mirror that ran from the floor to ceiling.

"Well—" Gustav begins to answer when the door to the laboratory flew open.

VoLt leaps into the room, landing on all fours, in attack position. He makes sure to make eye contact systematically with each of the four individuals in the room. Doctor Irvine, the most noticeably scared of the four, drops the clipboard from his hand as it crashes and rattles on the floor. Gustav and Zen are surprised to see VoLt, but strangely act calm by his sudden entrance, while the Kronox stands still with a sinister smile of anticipation.

"Did I come at a bad time?" VoLt asks.

"No, just in time, my old friend," Zen answers smoothly. He turns his attention to the Kronox and simply orders, "Attack."

The Kronox straightens his position and aligns himself squarely across the room from VoLt. Flexing his arms in an attempt to intimidate VoLt while displaying a large toothy canine smile, he utters, "This is going to be fun."

The Kronox starts to charge as VoLt begins to growl, displaying his own claws. Taking a step toward his adversary, he readies himself for impact. The blonde beast lowers his shoulder and delivers a thunderous tackle. The force pushes VoLt back toward the wall before he manages to shove the souped-up kronog off using both hands. The dog-like creature plants his feet and delivers a hard blow to the left side of VoLt's face. The impact momentarily brings VoLt down to one knee, but he manages to pop back up with a punch of his own to his assailant's lower left jaw. The Kronox steps back and he reaches up to his face in an effort to soothe whatever stinging VoLt caused.

Glaring at the lion-ape-like creature, the Kronox asks, "Is that all you got?"

Snarling, VoLt proceeds to deliver back-to-back punches that connect each time causing the Kronox's head to jolt back and forth side to side. VoLt's rapid action catches the creature off guard, until he manages to finally block VoLt's fourth attempt. The Kronox reaches with his right hand and grabs VoLt by the shoulder, only to grab his head and ram his face down to his own armored knee pad.

Pain shoots through VoLt's head as he finds himself down on his own knees, only to be propped up by his right arm. The Kronox proceeds to land a right-handed punch again to VoLt's face on his left cheek. VoLt stammers to get to his feet as the Kronox continues the attack.

Zen and Gustav watch in amazement as their creation appears to be getting the best of VoLt. Gustav holds the remote control device in his hand, but does not need to man any controls on it as his creature seems to be controlling the situation quite well on its own. Behind them, Dr. Irvine quietly tries to find a safe place to hide.

The battle finds VoLt with his back to the wall as the Kronox holds him by the neck. The blonde beast swings back to deliver another punch but instead, VoLt somehow musters the strength to land a quick jab of his own to the left temple of the Kronox. The dog-like creature releases his grip as VoLt manages to find inner strength to fight back. The kronog stumbles as he tries to gain back his balance. VoLt grabs the creature by his armored torso and flings him with all his might, causing him to go sliding across the cold metal floor, landing hard against the outer glass wall. The force causes the window to crack into a spider web form that slightly bows out.

VoLt II

Professor Zen glares at VoLt out of realization that VoLt might be getting the upper hand. Mr. Gustav looks down at his hand holding the remote control, as if forgetting that he had it in his hand. Zen, realizing that Gustav has the control, quickly orders, "Boost him!"

Gustav follows the orders and presses the blue button on the device which causes a noticeably blue electrical shock to shoot over the kronog's body.

The jolt causes the Kronox to let out a low rumble as he jumps to his feet. The creature turns his attention to Gustav and releases out a ferocious growl. VoLt stands still watching the creature react to the remote controlling device. The electric shock appears to generate from the metal armor plates that rests on his chest, legs, and arms.

Realizing that the armor plates were not just for protection but as an additional weapon, VoLt had to readjust his tactics in battling the dog-like creature. Cautiously moving in position for battle, he waits to see the Kronox's next move. The creature shakes off the electric tingling and refocuses on VoLt. For the first time, VoLt could clearly see the fiery red glow in the monster's eyes. Releasing a roar, the Kronox leaps in the air toward VoLt. Anticipating the attack, VoLt grabs the creature by the chest plate and flings him over his head using the momentum he already had. Planning VoLt's reaction, Gustav had his finger on the button that would send an electric shock once VoLt came in contact with it. Despite the fact that VoLt was able to defend himself from the flying attack, he still receives a strong jolt from the Kronox's armor.

The shock causes the muscles in VoLt's body to clench up uncontrollably as he stands frozen in muscle lock. Completely vulnerable, VoLt tries to focus on his adversary through the intense pain. He sees the kronog crouch down in attack mode and then charge at him. The violent impact causes the electricity running through VoLt to vanish, but it's too late for VoLt to react. The Kronox's impact came with such force that it sends VoLt flying out of the previously damaged window in a spectacular shattering of glass.

Simultaneously, Zen yells "No!" as he watches the Kronox throw VoLt out of the window. He runs to the gaping hole as he witnesses VoLt land hard on the adjacent rooftop roughly four floors below.

VoLt lands on his back, with his upper shoulders taking the blunt of the impact. Having the wind knocked out of him, he gasps for air. Panic starts to set in as he's afraid that he might pass out. Slowly, he starts to catch his breath, lying still for a moment as he tries to assess his new injuries. Feeling the urgency to move, he rolls over on his side, grimacing in pain. Still trying to get back to normal breathing, he looks up to the spot from which he fell.

Zen watches as VoLt gets to his feet and stammers to the far side of the rooftop before disappearing out of sight. The professor turns around and glares at his two business associates.

"Idiots!" he yells. "We had him!" He continues pointing to VoLt's last seen location.

"Go get him then," the Kronox sarcastically answers.

"That's what you're supposed to do!" Zen barks back.

"Hey, I asked for a game plan! I need more than just 'Attack!'" the blonde beast yells back as he pants heavily.

The creature then turns his attention back to Gustav with a scowl on his face.

"And what gives? Shocking me with that infernal device?" the Kronox asks.

He begins approaching Gustav in an apparent attempt to take the remote control away from him. Gustav quickly mans the device causing the Kronox to freeze in motion, only leaving him the ability to growl in anger. Mr. Gustav proceeds to work the device which causes the transformation of the Kronox back to Hank. Still frozen, Gustav walks over to Hank while looking Zen in the eyes with noticeable agitation. Without saying a word, he removes the chest, arm, and leg plates. Placing them on the laboratory table, he smoothly walks over back to the device and releases Hank from the electronic hold. Hank falls to the floor in pain, wincing, gritting his teeth.

As Jamerson lies on the floor, Gustav finally addresses Zen.

"I thought you would be pleased with the results. We all but had VoLt defeated! I believe we accomplished what we set out to do," Gustav says.

"I wanted to capture him!" Zen responds. "I need him!"

Zen slams his fist on the table.

"It was right there, practically in my grasp!"

"Why do we need VoLt? We have the Kronox," Gustav states.

"There's more to him than brute force," Zen replies, looking at Hank lying on the floor. He rolls his eyes as Hank attempts to stand up.

Hank uses the laboratory table to hold himself up. As he regains his normal strength, he looks the two square in the eyes, "I'm out. I've had enough of this."

Hank throws on his sweat pants, grabs his shirt, and proceeds to walk toward the service elevator.

"Where will you go?" Zen asks.

"None of your business!" Hank replies as he waits on the elevator.

"What do you think? You think you can simply just walk away from all of this? He knows who you are, and without the Kronox's powers, do you really think you have a chance?" Zen asks.

"I didn't sign up to be your trained dog!"

"And you're not a trained dog for your sports team?" Zen continues. "How long will that last? Soon, you'll be old news, nothing, working for scraps."

The elevator door opens, Hank stands there while he listens to Zen.

"We're offering you so much more. Power, wealth, longevity."

"Here?"

"No, not here. Why would you want to stay here? You could have your own island, women galore at your side. Sounds nice?" Zen asks.

"Where do we go from here?" an intrigued Hank asks.

"Where the money and resources are to build an army of soldiers like yourself, but you'll be the prototype, the benchmark," Gustav pipes in, indicating his buy-in into the plan.

"Right, where the money is!" Zen responds.

"So what's the game plan?" Hank asks as the elevator doors close without anybody getting on board.

CHAPTER 30

Gingerly, Dustin makes the long trek home. His body aches all over. Still holding his wounded ribs, he slowly walks up the seemingly monstrous flight of stairs to the main doors of the Berthel Church. Quietly as possible, he enters the sanctuary and makes his way to the front. As he approaches the front, he recognizes a figure sitting in the first pew. His shuffling feet catches the person's attention as he turns around.

"Dustin, you're back!" Pastor Phillips says with noticeable relief.

"Barely," Dustin responds as he plops down on the pew behind him.

"What happened?" Phillips asks, noticing the fresh new bruises and cuts on his face.

"Well, I found Hank and Zen, along with a fight."

Dustin tries to sit up as he explains the night's events to the pastor. Afterward, the two sit for a while, trying to determine their next move. Reluctantly, Dustin realizes that they may be in well over their heads.

"I think we might need help. Do you think your friend, Officer Hobbs, would be able to help?" Dustin asks.

VoLt II

Pastor Phillips didn't respond as the gravity of the situation starts to become apparent in his eyes.

The fog begins to lift as the streets ten stories below slowly appear from the window of the laboratory. Mr. Gustav and Professor Zen work feverishly as they try to gather as much information and supplies they can.

Acting with a sense of urgency and fearing that they had been reported to the authorities, Zen didn't want to take any chances of being caught again. Gustav sweats heavily as if his impending doom is at hand. Hank once again dons the metal chest plates and accessories in case duty calls. He stands over by the window looking down to see if the police were on the way.

"Are you sure Dr. Irvine went to the authorities?" Hank asks.

"Pretty sure," Zen answers, looking over various notes in Dr. Irvine folders.

"Why? Wouldn't he be in trouble too?"

"Not if he's cooperating," Gustav pipes in. "Do you see anything yet?" he asks Hank who stands watch.

"Can't really see, too foggy," Hank replies just as a hard knock pounds on the door.

"This is Detective Hobbs of Scotland Yard, we have a warrant for your arrest," the voice says behind the solid metal door.

Zen motions for them to move toward the service elevator in the back of the lab, just as the door comes flying open.

Detective Hobbs, holding his badge in one hand while pointing his gun with the other, yells, "Freeze! You're under arrest!"

Covering his face from being recognized, Hank crouches down behind Gustav and Zen. Then Gustav pulls the remote out of his pocket and presses the button triggering Hank's transformation.

Not sure what Gustav pulled out, one of the three officers that accompanied Hobbs takes a shot in Gustav's direction, which narrowly misses both Gustav and Hank. The newly transformed Kronox lets out a low roar as he emerges from the back of the laboratory and proceeds to advance toward the policemen.

"I said freeze!" Hobbs demands.

Another officer shoots at the Kronox as the bullet ricochets off of the metal plate. This only infuriates the creature as it lunges at the policeman, landing on him, causing him to fall on his back. Then the Kronox delivers a quick kick to the other officer, sending him into wall. Hobbs quickly aims his pistol at the Kronox, but the creature grabs his hand as he holds the gun and squeezes with all his might. Hobbs yells in pain as the creature kicks the remaining officer square in the chest.

Then the Kronox throws Detective Hobbs across the floor where he slides twenty feet before coming to a stop. The creature proceeds to pick up the officers one at a time, punching them square in the face, causing them all to go unconscious as blood trickles from their mouths and noses.

Turning back toward Hobbs, who is attempting to stand up, the beast attacks with fury. He delivers a hard blow to Hobbs's left jaw and then another to his right. The beast manhandles the fifty-year-old man with relative ease, but the creature doesn't let up.

"Please, have mercy," Hobbs utters.

Roaring in laughter at the detective's request, he picks up the battered man as he gasps for air.

"You want mercy? See a priest. I want VoLt!" the Kronox growls.

Minutes later, Hank crawls into the back of one of the LRSC delivery vans. Gustav is behind the wheel as Zen is in the back of the van as he explains the plan to Hank.

"Lay low, do you hear me?" Zen asks.

"Yeah, I guess, but where?"

"Don't care. When we need you, we'll call you." Zen says as he hands Hank his cell phone.

"What about you guys?"

"Don't worry about it," Zen answers in an annoyed tone.

Gustav calmly drives out of the building's garage and blends in with the traffic as distant sounds of sirens could be heard approaching the London Science Research Center. The van makes its way through the city until it finally reaches a quiet residential neighborhood. The back door opens and Hank jumps out.

"So, you'll be in touch, right?" Hank asks, looking like a dog that's being dumped alongside of the road.

"We're not done with you yet, boy," Zen replies as he tries to conceal his lack of confidence in his pet.

"Why can't I just stay with you guys?"

"Hank, everyone in town knows who you are. We need to find someplace under the radar until we can reestablish our plans. When we have things smoothed out, you'll hear from us," Zen replies.

Gustav gave a bewildered look to the professor, realizing that he had never heard Zen speak so kind to anyone before. Truly Zen had more invested in Hank than he had led on to believe.

"It'll be fine, Hank," Gustav responds, giving Hank a small reassuring smile.

The doors slam shut on the van as it pulls away, leaving Hank on his own. Looking concerned about his situation, he glances around the neighborhood. He seems to know the neighborhood quite well as he makes his way to a particular apartment building. A couple of the local residents populate the sidewalks and seem to be minding their own business, unaware of the celebrity who stands in their midst. The look on Hank's face reflects a man who wished he had the ability to blend in with the crowd and have a normal life, a far cry from the fame and fortune that he sought out to obtain. The paleness of his face and wide-eyed expression relays his urgency to get inside soon before he is spotted. He enters the building and races upstairs to the second floor. Knocking on a door, he rubs his gut. Despite the predicament he finds himself in, his internal clock seems to know it was nearly noon, and the rumble in his stomach indicates that the tank is all but empty.

CHAPTER 31

A light mist falls as Dustin steps out of the Underground subway system. Still feeling some pain with each step, he knows that he has to mask his condition as he makes his way toward Ginger's apartment. His heart races as he prepares himself to answer Ginger's impending questions regarding his whereabouts since abruptly leaving the hospital.

Looking both ways before crossing, he walks to the other side of the street as quickly as he could. Glancing up, he sees the light coming from her window as he approaches the stairs to her apartment building. Once inside, he climbs the one flight of stairs and knocks on her door. Hearing the quick approaching footsteps, he almost freezes in fear as he holds his breath.

The door opens. He can see the widening of her eyes.

"Dustin!" she yells as she quickly steps out and hugs him. "Where have you been?"

Gritting his teeth through her embrace, he lets out a small whimper.

"You're still injured!" she says as she quickly pulls back to look at him in the face.

"Just a little tender," he replies as he tries to put on a small grin.

She continues with a quick glance to check his appearance, softly touching his left jaw, noticing the new bruises to his face.

"I don't recall seeing these bruises while you were in the hospital," she states of her examination.

"Yeah, just a delayed reaction I guess," he responds. He couldn't help but feel a little touched by the fact that she had remembered his exact condition before he fled from the hospital.

"Where have you been?" she asks again.

"First, I'm sorry that I disappeared the way that I did, but I had to get out," he responds. "I had some business to tend to."

"In your condition?" she asks in a skeptic tone, "Were you able to help out your student?"

"What?" Dustin asks, as a sudden flush of embarrassment came over him.

"Yeah, that young man that came to the church while we were there," she pauses, "together."

"Cameron?"

"Yes, Cameron."

A sudden sense of panic runs up and down his spine.

"Oh, yeah…" His face turns pale white. "Crud. I forgot all about him."

Dustin quickly starts to weigh the consequences of not being there for Cameron when he needed him. Guilt begins to consume him.

"Then what were you doing?"

"I, uh, I was trying to figure out what attacked us," he answers without really realizing he was answering it.

His mind is focused on Cameron and the plight that he seems to be consumed in.

"Couldn't you just leave it up to the authorities to figure out?"

"Yeah, but I had to follow a hunch of mine," Dustin said.

He starts to refocus his mind on the conversation at hand.

"Well, did you find anything out?" Ginger asks.

"Well," Dustin begins to answer, when something stops him from continuing.

Coming out of the kitchen with a large sandwich in his hand and a huge bite in his mouth, the behemoth, Hank, approaches the two of them. Wiping the remnants of the sandwich that didn't make it into his mouth, he glances over Dustin's appearance and lets out a small chuckle, spraying bits of the sandwich over Dustin.

"Whoa, somebody did a number on you?"

Numbness comes over Dustin at the realization that Hank, the very man he had been battling, stood right in front of him.

"Man, did you find out what did this to you?"

Totally caught off guard and feeling a bit of fear run through his veins, he quickly re-tracks from his initial prepared speech.

"Uh, well, actually, I didn't find anything," Dustin said. "Just a wild goose chase."

"Boy, he really whipped you good, didn't he?" Hank replies as he looks over the hampered physique of Dustin.

"Yeah, I guess you can say that."

Dustin's stomach turns at the realization that Hank is taking such delight of his own handiwork. Fear begins to be replaced with anger at Hank's own smugness. Dustin wishes he had the medallion with him. He didn't care if his secret would be exposed. He wanted Hank to pay and to pay severely. His head starts to pound as blood rushes throughout his body.

"Hopefully the monster will get his own soon," Dustin replies, almost in shock that he said it, but nonetheless glad he had the courage to say it.

"What do you mean?" Hank asks.

"You know, just what goes around comes around," Dustin responds as he gives Ginger a look as if questioning why Hank is here in her apartment.

"Yeah, whatever. He's seems pretty tough to beat if you ask me."

Noticing Hank's lack of consideration for Dustin's condition, Ginger intervenes, "That's enough, Hank! The man is injured."

"Whatever."

"Seriously, Hank. Have some manners," she demands.

Hank looks at Ginger, as if recalling a conversation about his selfish personality as he receives her glare.

"You're right," Hank said. "You're right. Glad you're doing better, man."

Hank proceeds to slap Dustin on the back of the shoulder in a semi-friendly gesture which only sends jolts of pain through Dustin's body.

"Thanks," Dustin replies in a flat, unwelcoming tone.

Hank turns and walks back into the kitchen to finish devouring whatever he can.

Ginger turns her attention back to Dustin and mouths the words, "Sorry."

"What happened?" Dustin mouths back as he gestures toward the kitchen where Hank can be heard rifling through the refrigerator.

"I'll tell you later."

"Sure," he says as he slightly rolls his eyes. "Anyway, I guess I better be going."

The last conscious moment he had with Ginger was when they were walking arm in arm just before the kronog intervened. Now, all of a sudden, Hank's back in the picture. Feeling dejected, he gives Ginger a quick wave and starts to head out the door.

"Dustin," she says softly, so that Hank couldn't hear her. "You don't understand, it's complicated."

"Tell me about it," Dustin counters back as he closes the door behind him.

CHAPTER 32

Overlooking Hyde Park from the luxurious apartment of the drug dealer, Ronnie Griner, Professor Zen gazes out the window, arms folded. Ronnie sits at a bar stool next to the kitchen counter, looking around his living room at his uninvited guests. Mr. Gustav walks around the room, cell phone in hand, making several phone calls. When he is speaking to someone, he talks in his native tongue.

They arrived at five o'clock that morning, disturbing a peaceful night of sleep for Ronnie. They informed him they needed to wait it out until the pressure from the authorities had subsided. They recently discovered that Dr. Irvine did go to the police and notified them that they were conducting unlawful practices regarding human steroid consumption. Zen and Gustav informed Ronnie that they will be using his flat as their temporary headquarters until they could get reestablished at another location, however long that might take.

Gustav proceeded to make it clear that if Ronnie felt that they were impending on him, then perhaps the authorities would be interested in hearing about his profitable business as well. Reluctantly, Ronnie decided to be accommodating to his new tenants for as long as they needed.

Mr. Gustav hangs up his phone and approaches Zen at the window.

"They'll have a jet for us here tomorrow night."

"Tomorrow night?" Zen replies. "That doesn't leave us much time!"

Ronnie lets out a quiet sigh of relief after hearing of their impending departure.

"And what about our pet? Have you talked to him lately?" Zen asks regarding Hank.

"No," Gustav replies.

An eerie silence fills the room. Gustav paces the room slowly, as if trying to figure out their next move. Rubbing his beard and then letting out a stressed sigh, he turns his head in Ronnie's direction.

"Ronnie, can you turn on the television?" he asks.

"Uh, yeah, sure," Ronnie answers as he jumps from his seat to retrieve the remote control.

Turning on the seventy-two inch plasma television, the last channel he previously watched came on, BBC Sports. The three men stand still as the sports report comes on with an image of Hank "The Tank" Jamerson in the upper right hand corner. The sports anchorman in mid-report spoke frankly. "Authorities are currently looking for Hank "The Tank" Jamerson in regards to the incident at Scotland Yard from last week and as well as the recent incident at the London Science Research Center. We have reports that the Tank may be involved. There is also mounting evidence that Jamerson has been using highly enhanced steroids for some time. The sports commission is looking into these allegations. If this is true, then the London

Knights' world championship title could be tarnished. A stunned city has many calling for Tank Jamerson to turn himself in. Now, whether or not Jamerson is one of these 'kronogs' has yet to be proven. But one person perhaps has coined a new, more appropriate name for Hank Jamerson, saying he should be called 'Tankroid'."

Zen raises an eyebrow and rubs his chin with his right hand.

"Well, this changes things," he says.

Mr. Gustav looks at the television with an annoyed look as it appears his protégé continues to create more problems than bring solutions.

Hank looks at the television with a blank stare as the news came on. Remote still in hand, and mouth full of chips, he sits almost frozen in the brown leather recliner, watching the news report on him. Finally reminding himself to chew, he pops up from the chair and stands in front of the television.

"How in the bloody world?" he asks as the crumbs from his snacks fall off his shirt and onto the floor.

Enraged panic seems to come over him as he turns around to find a stunned Ginger standing behind him in the doorway of the living room.

"Hank?" she asks with a terrified look on her face.

"I can explain, trust me!" he replies, holding his hands out in front of him, almost pleading Ginger not to jump to conclusions.

"Is this true? Tankroid?" Ginger asks.

Hank shakes his head no in a manner that he needs to get a handle on the situation. He glances back at the TV screen. "Tankroid? Really? That's sounds like some infernal Pokémon character," Hank says in response to his new alter ego's name.

"Really, Hank? Focus!"

"All right, all right! You're right!" he says, turning back around to Ginger. "Like I said, let me explain!" he replies as the anger begins to quickly well up inside him.

CHAPTER 33

Dustin walks the streets for hours, trying to make sense of everything. He wants to pray, but he doesn't know what to pray for. Evil was building an army around him. The last encounter with the Kronox had him questioning whether or not VoLt could overpower him. The beast was so strong and so relentless.

"How do you fight something that has no remorse?" he asks himself.

Even as VoLt, with the enormous strength he has, he still has control, compassion, and a desire to help whoever it is that he confronts. He might fight his adversaries with everything he has, but the goal is to get them in a position where he can release them of the evil that consumes and controls them.

But this was Hank, the one man that he probably despised more than anybody in the world. Dustin knew it was wrong to carry so much hate for someone, but he couldn't let go of it. Was it jealousy and lack of confidence that fueled this strong dislike for Hank? Sure it was. He knew that much. Even if he didn't want to admit it.

Now, the fact that Hank had obtained special kronog powers that appears to be equal to his own had him questioning himself that much more. He wants Hank Jamerson to just fall of the face of the earth.

Then there's Ginger. If Hank would ever truly be out of the picture one day, what kind of future would they have? Dustin didn't want to be the consolation prize. He wanted Ginger to love him and accept him for who he is, and not just the guy there on the rebound. Her safety net, her casual date until something better came along.

A lot of negativity ran through Dustin's heart, soul, and mind. He found himself walking through Hyde Park, his head looking down most of the time. He happens to glance up, seeing a couple walking arm in arm, totally captivated by each other, drowning out the rest of the world around them.

"Yep, that's all I want," he says to himself.

He wants happiness, and right now, that didn't seem to be what God had planned for him.

A flood of guilt comes over him. He finds a park bench and sits down. Dustin waits for a moment as a group makes their way past him. As soon as they are a safe distance, Dustin buries his face in his hands.

"Dear Lord, help me!" he begins, "Forgive me for the hate I carry, forgive me for the insecurities I have, and forgive me for leaving you out so much in times that I really need you."

He pauses to wipe away a tear, "I just need you now. I don't know what to do. Please guide me. Please help me."

Dustin looks up to see a small break in the clouds that allow a small hint of blue behind them. "In your name I pray, Amen."

Dustin stands up, and rolls his shoulders from the slouchy posture that he had been keeping. He makes a mental note to straighten his back and hold his head up as he begins to walk home. Even if he didn't have all the confidence he needed for this journey, he might as well look like he did.

The look on Ginger's face shows utter disbelief as the news report connects Hank to the prison break of Professor Lucas Zen. Hank stands still behind her as he rolls his eyes over this predicament in which he finds himself.

She glares at him with a look of total disgust. "Who is this Lucas Zen?"

Hank closes his eyes and shakes his head no, as if indicating that part wasn't that important.

"Gin, just let me explain," Hank pleads as his face is plastered on the television screen with the tag "Wanted for Questioning" as it runs across the bottom of his sports image.

"Okay, I'm listening," she responds with her arms crossed and foot tapping, along with a questionable glare on her face.

"This guy approached me and asked me if I wanted a little bump. You know, to give me an extra push of energy."

Like previous arguments before with Ginger, Hank manages to cover his mistakes or discretions with half-truths and absurd stories that she wouldn't even bother questioning. This time, though, his back was against the wall. His world was crashing around him. His celebrity status appeared to be changing from famous to infamous in a blink of the eye.

"And you just took it?" she asks with her arms spread out, questioning his common sense.

"You don't understand!" Hank shouts back as he turns around, wanting to storm off.

"Oh, I understand! I understand that my boyfriend is a fraud, a cheat, and now a criminal!"

Turning around to face her, anger fills his eyes. Ginger continues her rant.

"And it's just not you affecting you! This is going to affect me! This is going to affect your team, and your friends!"

"You don't understand! I don't have any control!" he roars as he pounds his chest with his fist.

"You never had control!" Ginger shouts back. "You've always acted without thinking."

She pauses for a second as her eyes widen and her mouth gaps open as pieces started to come together.

"And it was you that nearly killed Dustin the other night."

Hank just glares off in the distance.

"What did Dustin ever do to you?"

"He's a twerp. Always has been, always will be," Hank answers. "He's been looking for an opportunity to weasel his way in."

"Really? Really?" she asks with her hands back on her hips. "It wouldn't be that he'd seen you do a lot of things that he knew I wouldn't be pleased about?"

"I knew I couldn't trust him. What all did he tell you?" he demands.

"Nothing, but you just did," she replies. "I want you out. I'm done."

"Where am I supposed to go?" Hank asks as he gestures to the television.

Ginger didn't respond, she just turned her attention back to the television report. Panic appears to set in as Hank realizes that he has few options.

"Ginger, you're right. I messed up. I need help," he pleads.

Hank turns around as if trying to think of something to say to help his situation when his cell phone rings.

"Oh, great," Hank responds noticing the caller ID on his phone.

"Yeah!" he answers.

"How's that fame and fortune working for you know?" Gustav replies from the other end.

"Great, just great! What do I do now?" Hank asks as he peers out the window, noticing cars parked outside that weren't there the last time he peeked out.

"Can you sneak out undetected?" Gustav asks.

"Possibly."

"Possibly? If you can't for sure, then you're on your own."

"Okay, okay, okay! I can get out." he responds, looking at Ginger with pitiful eyes in an attempt to lure her help.

"Okay, here's the plan," Gustav replies as Hank listens carefully to his instructions.

A black Jaguar sedan drives slowly down an alley behind Ginger's apartment building. The heavily tinted windows hide whoever might be behind the steering wheel. The basement door of the building cracks open cautiously as the car approaches. Looking around, Hank quickly bolts out the door and runs up the old concrete steps away from the basement floor and hops in the back of the spotless black car.

"Go, go, go!" Hank shouts as he looks at the driver.

"Relax, Tank," the driver responds. "Slow and steady wins the race."

"What?" Hank asks as he realizes he knows the voice. "Ronnie, is that you?"

"Yeah, it's me," Ronnie answers unenthusiastically.

"Man, am I glad to see you! Let's get out of here!" Hank says.

"It's not that easy," Ronnie replies calmly as he cautiously drives down the alley, trying to avoid anybody that might be looking for his passenger.

"What do you mean?"

"I have Zen and Gustav at my flat!" Ronnie says with noticeable agitation. He quickly lets out a heavy sigh as he tries to keep his cool in check. "They're waiting on us there."

"What's the plan?"

"Supposedly you three have a jet coming in to take you guys away," Ronnie states as he calmly turns onto a street and successfully blends in with the other traffic. "As far as I'm concerned, it can't come soon enough."

CHAPTER 34

Pastor Phillips enters the lobby of the hospital. It is his third trip to the hospital in four days. He looks exhausted as he approaches the reception desk to get the room number for Detective Arnie Hobbs. Thanking the receptionist for the information, he turns and proceeds toward the elevator. The weight of the world appears to be on his shoulders as he drags his feet across the lobby's floor.

He arrives on the third floor and makes his way to room 323. Knocking on the door, he slowly opens it and peeks in. Looking around the room, he makes eye contact with Arnie's wife, Carol. Upon seeing Jack's face, she releases a heavy breath at the recognition of their pastor. The corners of her mouth drop and tears suddenly appear in her eyes. She slowly stands up and greets the pastor. He reaches for her hand while he lays his other hand on her shoulder.

"I'm so sorry, Carol. How's he doing?" he asks.

"Better now. It was touch and go yesterday, but his vitals are improving," Carol answers, trying to keep her lip from quivering. "They don't know what did this to him. They think it might be one of those kronog creatures."

"It looks that way," he replies calmly as he looks at Arnie.

"What?" Carol answers with a sense of surprise that the pastor seems to recognize this type of beating.

"This was done by something mean, something that doesn't have remorse."

"What is it?" she asks.

Turning his attention from Arnie for a moment and looking Carol straight in the eyes, he replies, "Evil, pure evil."

"He just caught me on a bad day," Arnie replies in a low raspy voice.

The eyes of Carol and Pastor Phillips widened at the realization that Arnie is awake. They quickly go to his side as tears trickle down Carol's cheeks.

"Oh, Arnie, thank God you're awake!" she says as she kneels down, caressing his head and kissing his forehead.

"Just a minor setback," he replies with a small smile. He looks over at Pastor Phillips who stood there with a relived look on his face. "Hey, Jack."

"Hey, Arnie."

The pastor reaches down and squeezes his foreman, "I'm so sorry."

"I'm going to let the nurse know that you're awake," Carol says as she stands up. Leaning over, she kisses him again, softly on his bruised cheek.

Once she steps out of the room, Arnie turns his attention to the pastor.

"I could have used some help with that thing."

"He's trying to."

"Is he trustworthy?"

Jack pauses for a moment, seemingly reflecting on VoLt's character.

"Very," the pastor says of his young associate.

Carol re-enters the room with the nurse behind her.

"Well, it's good to see you're awake, Detective Hobbs," the gray-headed nurse says as she reaches for the chart at the end of his bed.

The nurse begins charting his vitals and checking his IV fluids. The wrinkles on the pastor's forehead indicate his concern for his friend's condition. He stays while the nurse assesses Arnie's condition.

"Okay, I'll go and page your doctor and let him know the improvements," she says with a reassuring smile.

A feeling of relief could be felt in the room. Noticing the level of stress on Carol's face, Jack didn't want to disturb the Hobbs's time together so he seized the moment to make his departure. "I'll be back to check on you in a bit."

"Sounds good. Thanks for coming in," Arnie responds.

"Thanks for coming in, Reverend," Carol says as she stands by Arnie's bed.

"Not a problem."

Dustin walks up the cold stone steps of the Berthel Church. It isn't until he reaches the top step that he realizes how sore his feet are. He had spent most of the afternoon and evening wandering around the city. Consumed with anger and rejection, he ponders his future with Ginger.

Looking up at the church, his mind was suddenly reminded of Cameron's situation. A cold rush comes over him at his realization of his forgetfulness.

"Man, what is wrong with me?"

He stands just outside the church doors, pondering the situation. Guilt consumes him for dropping the ball on Cameron's predicament.

"How do I handle this, Lord?"

He enters the sanctuary and makes his way to his quarters. Glancing down the hallway that runs behind the main auditorium, he notices the pastor's office door is open. Dustin decides to check in with the pastor before returning to his room.

As he reaches the opened door, he sees Sharon standing at the pastor's desk, watching the small television. A news report is playing, and it appears to have Sharon captivated.

Dustin taps on the door frame to get her attention.

A little startled, Sharon turns around to see who it could be.

"Dustin!" she shouts. "Oh thank God you're okay!"

She trots over and gives Dustin a hug.

"You are okay, aren't you?" she asks, noticing his cautious embrace back to her.

"I'm a little sore, but I'm okay."

"Did you hear about Arnie Hobbs?" she asks.

"No, what?"

Her tone caused his stomach to drop.

"He was attacked by the same creature that did this to you."

"What?"

Concern floods Dustin's mind as he wonders how Detective Hobbs got involved.

"And then it turns out that Hank Jamerson, you know, the sports star, is the creature that has been terrorizing the city!" Sharon reports.

"What?"

Dustin couldn't believe what he was hearing. He had been wandering around in the city all day, totally detached from the world around him, while all heck breaks loose.

"Where's Pastor Phillips?" he asks.

"He's at the hospital, visiting Arnie," Sharon replied. Noticing the concern on Dustin's face, she asks, "Is there anything I can do?"

"No, thanks." Looking down at the ground, trying to process all the information, he says, "I think I'm going to lie down for a while."

"I can only imagine how you feel," Sharon says. Shaking her head in disbelief, she asks, "What's going on out there?"

"I don't know." He pauses as another issue came back to the front of his mind. "If you need anything, I'll be in my quarters," Dustin says as he turns to make his way to his room.

"Same here, dear," Sharon responds. "If you need anything, just let me know."

It brought a little bit of peace to Dustin's mind knowing that between the pastor, Sharon, and himself, they each had each other's back, whether or not they knew the mess they were in.

VoLt II

Dustin takes a deep breath as he starts to strategize his efforts to aid Cameron. Once he reaches his room, he finds his address book and begins searching for Cameron's phone number.

CHAPTER 35

Inside a busy police station, Officer Green guides Ginger to an empty chair in front of his desk.

"Please have a seat," the officer says.

Ginger slowly sits down as she glances around the precinct. The large room is filled with roughly thirty desks, most of them occupied by other officers and other individuals, but she notices that she seems to have nearly everyone's attention. Her wrinkled forehead and wide-eyed expression displays a feeling of uneasiness. They all recognized her as the girlfriend of Hank Jamerson, the city's number one suspect at this moment.

"Okay, Miss Nevine, when's the last time you've seen or spoken to Mr. Jamerson?" Green asks.

"He was at my flat today," she answers in a frightened tone.

"He was at your flat today?"

"Yes."

"Did you know that he was wanted by the police?"

"I didn't until I saw the news reports this afternoon."

"And you didn't call us?

"No, I was, just so, mad," Ginger replies as her tone begins to change from fear to solid control as she starts to give him the details. "Once I saw that he was wanted for questioning, I told him to leave."

"Do you know where he is now?"

"No. He received a phone call and escaped out into the alley from my building's basement."

"Do you know who called him?"

"No, I don't."

"Are you sure?"

"Officer Green, it's becoming apparent to me that there are a lot of things in Hank's life that I was unaware of. And now I realize, the less I know, the better off I am."

Ginger continues to provide information she had regarding Hank. Realizing that her safety is a concern, the officer asked her if there was anybody she could call that she could stay with for a while.

She begins biting her fingernails as if pondering who she could contact.

"We could try Dustin Albatrose," she says with a bit of hesitation.

Dustin waits impatiently in the sanctuary for the doors to open. Glancing down at his watch, he knows that he better acquire some patience soon. After all, the person who he waited on had all the patience in the world, and Dustin had taken that for granted.

The doors finally open and a silhouette of a young man slowly approaches Dustin. His heart races as he knows he will have to work hard to gain this person's trust back. As soon as the figure closes in, Dustin begins to speak.

"Cameron, I am so sorry. I have no excuse for leaving you hanging like that."

Cameron approaches with a stern look, but soon releases the hard creases in his forehead when he sees the visible injuries to Dustin's face.

"What happened to you?" Cameron asks.

"Oh, I've just been living a little rough lately." Dustin replies, trying to put a lighthearted spin on the matter.

"Was it because of your friend, Ginger?"

"Partly, but that's not what I want to talk about."

Dustin could see Cameron put up the mental blocks between them.

"What do you want to talk about?" Cameron asks in a cold demeanor.

"Jayden, I want to talk about Jayden."

"I'm glad you remembered her name."

That one stung, he deserved that one.

"Cameron, I'm truly sorry. You're right. I've let you down. I want to make it up to you. Let me help you help Jayden."

The emotion begins to well up in Cameron's eyes as Jayden's situation comes to surface.

"It may be too late."

"What can you tell me?"

Reluctantly, Cameron begins telling Dustin everything he knew about Jayden.

"There's these thugs, you see. They have this thing that they are holding over Jayden. She can't escape it. She thinks she has no ability to fight it. Jayden doesn't think she matters to her family or anybody. She says that this is just her lot in life. That nothing is ever going to work out in her favor."

The pain in those words is so real to both Cameron and Dustin. Each of them had experienced that sense of loneliness, that sense of despair. Dustin realizes the dire situation that Jayden appears to be in. Action needs to be taken.

Dustin and Cameron spent the next hour discussing Jayden and agree that they would do whatever they could to save her. They finished their meeting in prayer.

Dustin was pleased the see the smile on Cameron as they wrapped up the conversation. Hope seems to have reemerged in Cameron's face.

"I'll see what I can find out, and then we'll plan out our next move, okay?" Dustin says.

"Okay, sounds good." Cameron replies. "And if you don't mind me saying, I think you should stay away from that Ginger Nevine lady. I don't think she's very good for you."

"Point taken."

Dustin follows that remark with a small smirk as Cameron excuses himself. Dustin wasn't too sure what to make of Cameron's last statement. Just an observation on Cameron's part, or was he allowing someone else to speak through him? Regardless, the statement had merit.

As Dustin made his way to his quarters, he hears the church phone ring. Reluctantly, he walks down the hallway and answers.

"Berthel Church, how may I help you?"

"Is Dustin Albatrose available?" the stern voice requests.

"Speaking. Who may I ask is calling?"

With raised eyebrows and wide eyelids, he awaits the response.

"This is Officer Green. I have Ginger Nevine here. I was wondering if you could come down to the station, please?"

Now the previous suggestion from Cameron was ringing loudly in his ears. How do you stay away from someone who won't let you go?

"Yes, sir, I'll be down shortly."

Dustin hangs up the phone and rubs the temples of his forehead with his right hand.

"I can't catch a break here."

CHAPTER 36

Evening had set on the city as Dustin steps off the Underground subway and follows the rest of the crowd up the stairs and out of the subway station onto the streets just outside Scotland Yard. He couldn't believe his predicament, having to come to the police station to retrieve his friend, Ginger. He knows that the police had wanted to speak to him regarding his encounter with the kronog, as the news reporters have recently connected him with Hank "The Tank" Jamerson. He just didn't feel up to the interrogation.

Dustin walks up to the receptionist's desk, heart racing. "I'm Dustin Albatrose. Officer Green called me. I'm here to pick up Ginger Nevine."

The fifty-year-old female officer kept her robot-like demeanor as she scans down at her clipboard, searching for the correct phone extension.

"One moment, sir," she replies as she dials the number. "Yes, Officer Green, Dustin Albatrose is here."

The unemotional receptionist listens intently, "Yes, sir…Yes, sir…Thank you, sir."

She hangs up the phone and points to the row of chairs to the left of her that ran along the wall of the lobby.

"Have a seat and Officer Green will be here to take you back," she says without making eye contact.

"Take me back?" Dustin replies, as it sounded like he was heading to certain doom.

"Yes," the receptionist responds.

"Okay," he says as he walks over to the row of chairs and sits down.

Dustin sits down in the hard plastic seat with cold chrome legs that were connected to the rest of the eight lined chairs. The intensity of the situation runs through his body, causing the muscles in the neck and back to tighten, making sitting in the hard cold chairs that much more unpleasant. His eyes scan the area continuously, wondering where the next attack will come from.

"Are you Albatrose?" Detective Green asks.

Dustin quickly snaps his head in the direction of the stern voice.

"Uh, yes, sir."

Dustin feels a little embarrassed of his jittery response.

"Come on back," Green says as he quickly turns around, fully expecting Dustin to follow his orders, which he did. "I'll get you a cup of coffee. Might warm you up."

They reach Green's desk where Ginger greets Dustin with a soft, "Sorry about this."

Dustin just gives her a blank look as he mentally prepares himself for questioning.

The detective comes back with a cup of coffee and hands it to Dustin.

"Here you go, hope you like it black."

"Uh, sure, thanks," Dustin replies as he takes the cup from the officer. Blowing it before taking a sip, he prepares his taste buds for the staunch flavor that was about to come their way. Normally, he likes sugar and cream in his coffee, when he drinks it, which he seldom does. As for this moment, he wasn't about to ask for anything extra.

The coffee was even stronger and hotter than he anticipated as he took a sip.

"So, I understand that Hank Jamerson, or Tankroid as they are calling him, attacked you a few days ago?" Green asks.

"Tankroid?" Dustin asks with bulging eyes, trying to fight off a smile. "Isn't that a name of a Pokémon character?"

Ginger's eyes widened at Dustin's remark.

"Well, I, uh, don't know about the name's origin, son. But back to the important question, is he the one that attacked you the other night?" Green asks with a slight hint of agitation with Dustin's ill-timed humor.

Dustin quickly sits up and promptly answers the question with respect for the officer.

"Well, I can't be for sure, but it might be."

A sudden rush of heat runs up and down Dustin's spine as the officer doesn't waste any time with his next question.

"What did he look like?"

"Well, honestly, it happened so fast. I don't really remember seeing anything," Dustin says as he answers as truthfully as he can. He knows he has the opportunity to seal Hank's fate, but he can't bring himself to do it.

Officer Green didn't respond. He just stares at Dustin with robot-like eyes. Feeling completely uncomfortable, Dustin squirms slightly in his seat as the soreness in his body keeps him from finding a position that didn't trigger some kind of ache in his body.

Letting out a heavy stream of air through his nostrils, Green appears to realize that he isn't going to get that much out of the young man. Leaving his robotic demeanor, he tilts his head to the side and leans back into his chair.

"All right, well, looks like you're still in the state of recovery," Green says.

Dustin nods his head in agreement.

"Okay," the officer responds as he sits back up. He reaches up and grabs one of his business cards from his desk and hands it to Dustin. "If you don't mind, when you start to recall any specifics of those events, I'd be interested knowing them. If you're willing to share them, that is."

"Yes, sir."

Glancing back at Ginger while still addressing Dustin, the officer continues.

"Okay, well, Miss Nevine wanted to know if she could stay with you for a while? You know, until we find Mr. Jamerson."

"Oh, okay," Dustin replies, wondering how this is going to work.

"Very well then," Green says. "Now be careful. And Miss Nevine, we'll be contacting you if we need further assistance from you. The same may go for you, Mr. Albatrose."

"Okay," they both answer like two kids who were just sent to the principals' office.

"Very good then, you're dismissed," Green says.

The two slowly and humbly excuse themselves and leave the officer's desk. Dustin glances around the large office room and notices that Ginger once again has everyone's attention. Neither one of them says a word as they try to walk as calmly as they can as they leave the police station.

They walk for a couple of blocks under the city's streetlights, as Ginger finally vents her frustrations. Dustin has his own to vent, but for the moment, he needs to keep a few of those to himself. The cold air freezes the steam coming from Ginger's mouth as she rattles off her complaints.

"I just can't believe how stupid I was!" Ginger states. "All that was going on right under my nose and behind my back. And now, my job is in jeopardy at the BBC. They think I'm involved somehow, like I helped create this monster to conjure up my own 'VoLt' story. Can you believe that?" she says as she places her hands in the air.

"It's all hard to believe," Dustin replies.

"And to think, Hank nearly killed you, on purpose!"

"Yeah, there's that too."

"Ugh, I just want to vomit."

Dustin couldn't help but chuckle a little bit at her last statement.

"What?" she says in response to his small laugh.

He pauses as he ponders if she is truly ready for the question he had for her.

"Come on, what?" she pursues.

"Okay," he says as he stops walking to address her face to face. "Explain it to me, Gin. You tell me that you are done with Hank just before the kronog attacks me. Then, when I go to your flat, Hank's there acting as if nothing has changed between the two of you."

"I know, it looked bad, but believe me, we are done!"

"Yeah, I realize that now, but if all this about Hank hadn't come out, then what would have become of us?"

"Dustin?" she replies, indicating she hadn't had a chance to really think about it.

"Regardless of Hank, Ginger, where do I stand?"

"I don't know. All I need is my Dustin right now."

She gives him a little pouty face, seemingly trying to gain some sympathy from him. She grabs his wrist and playfully swivels back and forth, as she attempts to get him to play along as well.

Frustrated with her for dodging the question again, he feels the strain she is putting him through. He gently spreads his arms out which causes her to lose her grip. Ginger gives him a look of surprise as he resisted her charm.

"I don't think I can be here for you right now," Dustin replies.

He didn't take delight in the comment. He didn't feel bad for it either. It just felt like a huge weight had been lifted from his shoulders for finally telling the truth.

"What do you mean?"

Her arms seemingly locked in position from the break of her grasp of his wrists.

"I think you need to find 'you'," he replies.

"What?" Ginger responds, a confused, stern look coming over her face.

She brings in her arms and folds them close to her body as the cold air whips around her.

"You have been tied down to someone for the past six years. You're identity has been Tank's Tink."

"Hey!" she says angrily at the nickname.

"Hear me out, please!" Dustin demands. "That's what I mean. It's an identity that you got stuck with, it's the identity that you proudly carried around these past years, and it's the identity that got you your job as well as the identity that cost you your job."

Ginger didn't say anything. She just looks down at the ground, listening to him.

"You need to find your own identity before your current one costs you a friend," Dustin says.

Tears begin to form in her eyes. A sense of remorse starts to build in Dustin, but he has to tell himself to stand his ground. He can't fall victim to her puppy dog eyes again. It is for her own good that he stays firm on his request.

"Ginger, I know you can do it. You have to do it, and when you do, I'll be right here." He leans over and gives her a kiss on her forehead and walks away, leaving Ginger alone in the park.

CHAPTER 37

A couple of days pass, and Dustin is enjoying the peace and quiet for a change. Now that the authorities knew the true identity of Tankroid and his involvement with Gustav and Zen, Dustin wonders if his assistance would be needed anymore since the authorities seem to have them in their sights. Dustin meditates in prayer in his room. His thoughts and requests focus on Ginger and the situation with Hank. Not sure what he wanted himself, he just prays that God would guide him down the path he needs to go. As he listens for that small still inner voice, Cameron's dilemma comes to the forefront of Dustin's mind.

Suddenly Dustin's heart races as he realizes that God is speaking to him, letting him know that Cameron needs help.

"Forgive me, dear Lord. Be with me as I do your will. Amen."

Dustin shoots up from the bed and stands still for a moment as he ponders his next course of action. He quickly changes into his black running shorts and throws on a red running sport shirt. As he laces up his tennis shoes, he recalls Cameron stating that Jayden would often be found hanging out with a rough bunch of teenagers near Piccadilly Circus.

Grabbing his backpack and shoving his cloak and medallion in it, he proceeds to stretch his legs for a healthy run. As he stretches, he becomes aware of the soreness that still resonates in his ribs and back. His mind also reflects back to the doctor's request to "take it easy."

"I'll try to," Dustin softly says to himself as the leaves his quarters.

Stepping out of the church and with his backpack strapped on, he starts off in a light jog toward Piccadilly Circus.

"Ow," Dustin mutters softly as he feels his body react to the jog. It takes a couple of paces before his body settles in. He can feel the acute pain in his ribs. Focusing on his breathing, he powers through the soreness and continues on. As he runs, his thoughts go back to the previous conversation he had with Cameron regarding Jayden.

Jayden had been a member of this gang for a couple of years now. She lived with her dad, who wasn't home a lot, but when he was, he would often make life difficult for her. On one particular night, she felt she was in danger. Jayden's seemingly only option was to run away. Desperate to find shelter she ran across this gang and their ringleader, Pug. Longing to fit in somewhere, she found herself being accepted into this group. Unfortunately, this gang had a reputation for being involved in small petty crimes. Most of the time, they stole food and change whenever the opportunity presented itself. They quickly discovered that Jayden had a knack for pickpocketing as well as serving as a good decoy for bigger jobs. It was the first time in Jayden's life that she felt she had some kind of worth, even if it was law breaking at times.

Her situation became more involved when she was pegged by Pug to help pull a job in a pawn shop and steal jewelry for the gang. These jobs though were more than just a trick for the gang, in her mind. It had become a necessity for her "family." This had become a means to put food on their table.

But on this particular job, her involvement became much more serious. Pug and his self-selected group returned to a pawn shop that had proven to be lucrative for their needs in the past, but on this shopping spree, the owner was ready for the gang. It had become apparent the owner was on to their tactics.

The owner played cool as he let Pug, Jayden, and another decoy browse the store. Pug and his fellow gang member seemingly had the owner's attention when Jayden attempted to do her job.

With relative ease, Jayden was able to quickly reach behind the counter and grab a gold watch, when suddenly the store owner called her out.

"Put it down, missy!" the store owner barked.

Immediately releasing her grip of the gold watch, she turned her head toward the owner. Her eyes widened at the sight of the handgun the owner had aimed at her. She looked over at Pug who seemed to be locked in a dead stare with the owner.

"What are ya' goin' to do, shoot her?" Pug taunted.

"You all aren't pulling another trick on me anymore."

"Ah ya?" Pug paused. "Maybe you're right."

As quick as he could, Pug pulled a gun from his back and aimed it at the owner. But the owner didn't hesitate a second and fired a shot at Pug. Grazing his left shoulder, Pug quickly took aim and shot back, hitting the store owner square in the chest.

The owner gasped for air as he landed chest first on the counter, then proceeded to slide down behind it.

"Let's get out of here!" Pug ordered his associates.

Just as they were fleeing the scene, Pug saw the surveillance camera aimed right at them.

"Jayden, Stop!" Pug yelled.

"Why?" She yells back.

"I gotta get that tape!" he yelled back, pointing to the camera just above their heads. "Here!" Pug barked. "Hold this," as he placed the gun in her bare hands. Her mouth gapped open as she looked at the murder weapon in her own hands.

"Hurry!" Jayden replied. Her eyes were wide open as tears began to well up. She breathed heavily as she could hear Pug rummaging in the back. She turned her head to look at the surveillance camera, but as she stared at it, she began to follow the cable wire from it. She followed it to where it ran just behind the counter where the pawn store owner laid. Jayden took a deep breath and approached the counter, cautiously looking around it for the recording machine, all the while trying not to look at the murder victim. She found the VCR, located right under the counter as she suspected. Pushing the eject button, the VCR tape emerged. Taking it and hiding it in the back of her jeans, she quickly went back to the front of the store where Pug left her.

Panic began to set in.

"Pug?" she hollered.

Suddenly a loud crash came from the back, Jayden jumped out of fear from the sound of numerous items being knocked around. The commotion was quickly followed by a tirade of profanity flowing from Pug's mouth.

"The freakin' dude was a hoarder! Crap everywhere!"

"Did you get it?"

"No. I don't know where it could be."

Pug emerged from the back and stared at the same surveillance camera. Seemingly studying it, he too began following the cable cord back to the counter with the recording device resided. Quickly jumping to the device, he pushed the eject button and waited for the tape to pop out. When nothing happened, he pushed the eject button again.

"Gez, what a waste! He didn't even have a tape in it. What a loser, man," Pug said.

Jayden didn't respond. She just waited for his command to run.

Looking around the area outside the store's door window, Pug ordered, "Okay, let's go!"

It was soon afterward she learned that the gang had their own laws that kept the group intact. Pug didn't waste an opportunity to remind her of the grip he had over Jayden. If she would ever try to break from the group, he would rat her out to the police as the one who killed the pawn shop owner. After all, he had the weapon that had her fingerprints all over it.

"You think your life stinks now, just try living behind bars," Pug stated once to her.

She would be reminded constantly of that fact on a regular basis. She never told anyone in the gang that she had the videotape of the store owner's death. It was her security net. Despite the fact that Pug would routinely remind her of her involvement in the crime, the gang was the closest thing she had to a family.

Jayden only met Cameron on a chance encounter at the restaurant where Cameron's mom worked as a waitress. Cameron had recognized her as a girl from his school in which they shared a class together. Something about her seemed to captivate Cameron's attention. So much so that Cameron found himself attempting to start a conversation with her that night.

"Hey, I haven't seen you in class for a while," Cameron said.

Jayden looked a little surprised to be recognized by someone.

"Excuse me?" Jayden asked defensively. "Who are you?"

"I, uh, I'm Cameron. We share history class together."

Cameron was caught off guard by her own defensive tone. As he answered her, he could tell that she seemed to be preoccupied by the waitress up by the counter, where various dessert plates were set out.

Jayden looked back at Cameron as she seemed to make the connection with him.

"Oh, yeah, that's right."

She paused again as she seemed to stake out the desserts.

"You're, ah…?"

"Cameron, my name is Cameron."

"Yeah, that's right."

Jayden watched the waitress step away from the display of desserts. She looks back at Cameron for a quick second.

"Uh, sorry, gotta go," she said.

She quickly dashed to the counter and grabbed a blueberry muffin. She turned and looked at Cameron as she quickly and smoothly bolted for the door. She placed a finger to her lips in a gesture asking Cameron to be quiet. She smiled and ran out the door while Cameron sat still, completely captured by her.

A couple of days later, Jayden showed up to school, presumably by the request of the truant officer. She plopped down in her seat just before the class started. Cameron rushed into the room just as the bell rang. Taking a seat next to her, he turned to her and smiled. She returned a sarcastic smile back at him.

As he reached in his back pack to retrieve his books, he pulled out a muffin wrapped in a napkin and handed to Jayden.

"You should try the banana nut bread one, they're my favorite."

Jayden looked at Cameron with a surprised look and a genuine smile.

The two quickly formed a bond and began spending a lot of time together. But once Pug became aware of Jayden's attempt to distance herself from the gang, he began to tighten the ropes that bound her to the group.

Cameron pleaded with her to seek help. He even invited her to his Bible study class one night thinking that Dustin might have an idea as to how to help her. But unfortunately neither one found the assistance they needed that night at church.

Just days after their inability to find help, Jayden came to Cameron with tears in her eyes. She told him that Pug had threatened her to come back to the group or suffer the consequences. Distraught over possibly losing her, he went to see Dustin at the church for possible help, but instead, he found Dustin locked in arms with Ginger. After getting through the awkward moment, Cameron agreed to meet Dustin later that evening, but Dustin never arrived. And to make things worse, Cameron also hadn't seen Jayden since that night.

Dustin found himself in a strong, steady pace as the repercussions of his neglect of Cameron's pleads went unanswered. The busy traffic that populated the area around Piccadilly Circus forced Dustin to slow down his jogging pace. Glancing around the numerous clusters of people, he tries to find Jayden somewhere amongst the crowd.

As he stops at a traffic light and jogging in place, he hears a voice call out to him.

"Nice legs!"

"What?" he asks as he looks around to see who had just heckled him.

To his surprise, it is Jayden. She sits on the concrete steps of a building along with five other individuals. All dressed in various black attire and all sporting different colored hair and numerous piercings.

Stopping his jog, he turns to face Jayden about fifteen feet away.

"Thanks, Jayden. How are you doing?"

A look of shock comes over Jayden's face. Dustin didn't know if the look is from being recognized or from recognizing him.

"Oh, hey," she replies in a polar opposite tone from her heckling remark just moments ago. "I didn't know it was you."

By now, a man in black leather pants and a sleeveless shirt with green, spiky hair begins to eavesdrop on their conversation.

"Are you going to be there Wednesday night for Bible study?"

"I, uh…" she stammers.

Jayden looks a little uncomfortable with the conversation as the green spiky-haired man speaks up. "Bible class?"

The man stands up and begins to step in between them.

"It's nothing, Pug," Jayden says.

As Pug looks at Dustin, Jayden shakes her head no behind Pug's back. Dustin didn't know if it is a gesture that she wouldn't be attending his class or that she didn't want Dustin to get into a scuffle with Pug.

"Pug, is it?" Dustin asks with a small smile as he has to fight not to laugh at his name.

"Yeah, that's right."

He stands there with a smirk as he seems to be sizing Dustin up.

"Do I need to go through you to talk to Jayden?"

"Yeah, that's right."

The two stare each other down as Jayden finally comes to her feet and intervenes between the two.

"Pug, it's okay, I'm not going. That Cameron kid dragged me there last week. Don't worry, it won't happen again."

She turns around and looks Dustin in the face.

"Please go, before you get us all in trouble," she says as she places her hand on Pug's chest in an attempt to back him off.

"Is everything okay?" Dustin asks.

"This is as good as it gets for some of us."

Dustin could see the hopelessness in her face.

"Tell Cameron I'm sorry, but—" she started, but the reference to Cameron lit a fire in Pug.

"You heard her! Now buzz off!" Pug shouts.

Several pedestrians are starting to notice the verbal scuffle between Pug and Dustin.

"All right, all right." Dustin pauses.

Then looking at Jayden with the most serious eyes he could muster, he adds, "Jayden, if you need anything at all, you know where to find me."

Jayden nods slightly in agreement.

"I said take off, preacher boy!" Pug yells.

Dustin reaches up and squeezes the straps of his backpack with his right arm. He had to fight the urge to let his alter ego handle the situation. Reluctantly, Dustin slowly turns around and waits for the light to turn green to cross the busy street. Once across, he commences with his jog. Breathing heavily through his nostrils and mouth, it is all he could to do to keep from ripping off Pug's pierced ears, medallion or not.

His blood boils as he reaches Hyde Park. Trying to run out his frustration, a reoccurring question runs through his mind. Does being a Christian mean you have to be passive? As VoLt, he could act on transgressors of God's people, especially since he had the ability to release them of the controlling sin in their lives. But as Dustin, he felt restricted. He turned the other cheek in his own life on too many occasions. He just wished he could act on his own instinct and not suffer any ramifications, but in his line of work, there would always be ramifications.

Totally immersed in his thoughts as he jogs, his attention is drawn to a number of squad cars that suddenly appear in front of a luxury apartment building. The fact that they arrived without sirens blaring told him that they were planning on surprising whoever they were after. A sick feeling rolls in his stomach, a feeling that he knew who and what they were after. Quickly, he scans the area for a place to change.

CHAPTER 38

Overlooking Hyde Park on the sixth floor, Ronnie stands out on his balcony. Slightly turning and glancing back into his apartment, he looks at the uninvited guests who occupy his living room. He nervously taps his fingers on the balcony's railing, when a family in the park momentarily catches his attention. Ronnie watches as the family of three attempts to fly a kite. A small smile comes over his face, wishing he had a family to enjoy the smaller things in life. Quickly though, his attention turns toward a group of squad cars that pull up to the entrance of his building below him.

He lets out a small sigh and whispers to himself, "It's about time."

Ronnie walks in from the balcony and glances over his three guests. The television is turned off. Hank is sprawled out asleep on the couch in Ronnie's old gray sweat pants and white T-shirt. Hank had the sleeves and neck cut out to create a pitiful looking tank top. Mr. Gustav sits at the wet bar, talking on his cell phone in his native tongue, while Lucas Zen sits at Ronnie's computer tapping away. Quietly, Ronnie walks over to the kitchen which is closest to the front door, pretending to be searching for something in the cabinets.

Suddenly there is a harsh pounding at the door, which noticeably startles Gustav and Zen. Hank lies unaffected by it.

"This is the police, we have warrants for your arrest! Open up!"

"Well, it was a good run while it lasted," Ronnie says as he motioned toward the door.

"Don't open it, Ronald!" Zen growls.

Ronnie shoots a glare at Zen, seemingly annoyed at being told what to do in his own apartment.

"Whatever," Ronnie replies as he reaches for the doorknob.

Zen quickly grabs the remote control device and points it at Hank and presses several buttons.

Hank shoots up from the couch with a loud yelp as he finds himself transforming into the hideous Kronox, now known as Tankroid.

Seeing the terrifying creature transform, Ronnie quickly opens the door and falls to the ground, covering his head, allowing the authorities in.

As they cautiously entered the residence, the police see the Tankroid creature stand before them. Drawing their guns, one of the officers yells, "Freeze! You're under arrest."

By now, Zen is standing beside his kronog as he places his hand on his shoulder, "It's time to go."

The creature grabs Zen and flings him over his shoulder and walks out onto the balcony, with Mr. Gustav right behind them.

"I said 'Freeze'!" the policeman yells just as Mr. Gustav pulls out a gun from his holster inside his gray suit coat.

Without hesitation, shots are fired. Mr. Gustav is hit square in the chest as he flings back, hitting the glass window behind him, causing it to shatter. Falling through the shattered frame, Gustav falls flat on his back onto the balcony. One bullet grazes Zen's arm as another hits Tankroid in his right shoulder. Growling in pain, the creature manages to power through and hops to the balcony's railing. He lets out a roar which causes the police to temporary halt their approach. Seizing the moment, Tankroid, with Zen in tow, leaps to the balcony's railing of the floor above them, safely carrying Zen to safety.

"Good job, my boy. Can you keep going?" Zen asks Tankroid as they escape from the police's view.

"Yes," the beast responds without putting Zen down.

"Good. Then let's keep going."

Tankroid proceeds to climb up two more flights until they reach the roof.

"Where to now?" a calm and exhausted Tankroid asks.

"The shipping docks," Zen replies.

Gustav lies on his back, gasping for air as the police cautiously approach. Ronnie, already in handcuffs, watches as Mr. Gustav's condition is quickly assessed by the authorities.

"Better call an ambulance," one cop says as he stands up to look over the balcony's view only to see a large hairy creature quickly scale the side of the building and pop up onto the balcony's edge.

Officers scramble for their guns again as the massive creature climbs over the railing and lands on the balcony. VoLt just raises his hands in a gesture indicating that he means no harm. He stands still as he waits for the officers to make their next move. After a couple of tense seconds, one policeman slowly lowers his gun as he orders the other officers to do the same. VoLt lets out a sigh of relief as he slowly kneels down beside Mr. Gustav and looks him in the eyes.

The red glow is beginning to fade along with the life he has left.

Reaching down, VoLt places his hands over Gustav's face.

"What are you doing?" one officer shouts as he again raises his gun and aims it at VoLt.

VoLt glances up for a moment at the confused officer and then turns his attention back to Gustav.

"Repent," he softly mutters as he mysteriously consumes the evil from Gustav.

Gasping, Gustav looks up at the creature with surprised eyes and whispers, "Thank you."

VoLt glances around the room and sees all eyes watching him. He pauses as he battles an internal struggle for a moment. Then he bends down closer to him and grabs Gustav's hand.

"My Lord and Savior is Jesus Christ. If you accept him as your own, all your transgressions with be forgiven, and you will live forever in his kingdom once you leave this place." Looking in Gustav's eyes in his last moments, he asks, "Would you accept him as your Lord and Savior?"

"Yes," Mr. Gustav replies as his panting becomes quicker.

Then he squeezes VoLt's hand until his life is quickly gone.

VoLt rests the lifeless hand of Mr. Gustav back on his chest. Standing up and stepping back to the railing, he strains over the balcony's edge and looks toward the rooftop of the building.

As he readies himself to pursue Tankroid and Professor Zen, an officer shouts, "Don't move!"

VoLt slowly turns around, holding his arms up slightly, to see four policemen with their guns drawn and pointed at him.

"You're coming with us!" the officer in charge barks.

As the cop approaches VoLt with handcuffs, a voice from the doorway hollers. "Let him go!"

The cop turns around to see Detective Hobbs enter the apartment with a use of a cane. His dark brown trench coat bunches up on his right side as he struggles to get accustomed to his assisted walking device.

"Uh, Detective Hobbs, what are you doing here?" the cop asks as he continues to hold the handcuffs with intentions to place them on the creature's wrists.

"I said, let him go," Hobbs requests again with a stern look in his face. The policeman complies and places the handcuffs back on his belt.

As Hobbs approaches VoLt, he mans his walkie talkie and speaks into it, "Anything up there?"

"No, sir, all clear up here," the voice answers as it crackles on and off.

"We're too late," he mumbles under his breath as he places his communicator back on his belt.

Hobbs walks over to VoLt and leans in slightly and says to him, "You owe me one."

VoLt nods his head in acknowledgement as the bile begins to burn severely in his stomach. Detective Hobbs takes a step back and looks at VoLt, then nods his head in a gesture which told VoLt to leave.

"Thank you," VoLt responds as he makes his way across the apartment as the officers watch in awe. Once he exits the flat, he runs toward the stairway at the end of the hall.

A couple of the officers make steps to follow, but Hobbs orders them to stand down and allow the creature to go.

As soon as VoLt is safe in the stairwell, away from any eyes, he takes off the medallion and transforms back into Dustin. Still feeling the evil bile in his stomach, he knows he has to release it. Panic begins to set in, as he had never held in the bile for so long, let alone in his normal state. Feeling weak and sick, he runs down a flight of stairs to the next floor down. Feeling vulnerable in his cloak and running shorts, the urgency alerts him to find and hide in a place where he could vomit the evil fluid that boils in his belly.

He jogs down the hallway looking for anything that would aid him. To his relief, he finds the janitor's closet. Holding his breathe, he turns the knob and finds it unlocked. Letting out a sigh, he enters and locks the door behind him. Seeing a large sink amongst other various cleaning and maintenance supplies, he gives out a quick prayer.

"Oh, thank you, Lord!"

Taking off the cloak and running to the large sink inside, he releases the bile by throwing up. It is disgusting enough when he does this as VoLt, but the bile burned more and tasted worse in his normal human form. Instead of burning the bile away, he simply just washes it down the drain. The convulsion of muscles caused havoc on his sore diaphragm. He sits on the floor for a moment to catch his breath and regain some strength. Sweat pours from his forehead.

"Okay, so I'll only do that in my other state from now on."

He continues to spit the remnants in the sink until it is all but gone. Still wearing the backpack over his bare torso, he realizes that he is on borrowed time. He quickly takes off his backpack and digs out his red running shirt and tennis shoes and throws them on. Folding up the cloak and shoving it in the backpack along with the medallion, he instantly looks like a fitness junkie heading out for a jog.

Stepping out of the janitor's closet, he runs to the elevator and catches a ride down to the lobby. Taking deep breaths on the descent down, he tries to calm his nerves. The doors open to a bustle of activity as officers and media swarm the lobby. The elevator doors next to his open at the same time. Dustin glances over to see

Detective Hobbs limp off the lift. Hobbs looks over and makes eye contact with Dustin just as a slew of reporters begin to approach the detective. Amongst the flood of questions, Hobbs gives Dustin a slight nod of his head. Dustin returns the nod as a sudden rush of sweat begins to form on his temple again. A dam of thoughts breaks loose in Dustin's mind as he tries to decipher what the nod from Hobbs meant. Is it recognition of a fellow church member or a "I know your secret" nod? Regardless, Dustin discovers that he has enough adrenaline to fuel a legit run home.

CHAPTER 39

Night had overcome the city. The water from the River Thames brushes up the side of the concrete docks, causing splashes to drench the walkway. Cautiously aware of the surroundings, Professor Zen and Hank approach a cargo ship's ramp. Holding his right shoulder with his left hand, Hank had a brown coat thrown over his back in an attempt to cover his wound. Looking over the massive red-coated ship, he glances back to Zen as they proceed up the walkway.

"I thought we had a jet coming for us?" Hank asks.

"Change of plans," Zen answers.

"Are you sure they're expecting us?" Hank asks.

"Yes, Mr. Gustav made these arrangements just prior to his departure," Zen replies in a matter of fact tone.

Hank looks at the back of Zen with a concerned glare. Hank seemingly realizes that Zen is treating Gustav's death as more of a business departure than an actual death. He witnessed the professor's coldness toward others, never allowing emotions for others to interfere or exist. Professor Zen had a wicked mindset. Once he had an objective to reach, he would not let anyone or anything stand in his way.

A Middle Eastern man holding a rifle meets them at the top of the ramp. Standing firm, he asks them to identify themselves.

"My name is Professor Lucas Zen, and this is my associate, Hank Jamerson," he calmly replies. "I'm afraid that my business partner, Yuri Gustav, will not be joining us."

Looking over the two, the guard responds, "Very well. The captain is expecting you," he says with a heavy accent. The guard brings the gun down to his side as he guides them to the captain's quarters.

Captain Mustavich sits at his desk, determining a route on his map. A knock at the door doesn't interrupt his concentration.

"Yes?" he says.

The guard opens the door. "Captain, Professor Zen and his associate are here."

"Let them in," the captain replies as he notes a stopping point on the map, then looking up, he greets his new passengers.

"Welcome, welcome, come right in." the captain says, standing up.

Both Professor Zen and Hank size up the captain of Pakistani descent as they both scan him over from head to toe. Standing nearly eye to eye with Hank, his large girth made him a little intimidating to them. The captain's hat sits crooked on his head, while his smile is partially covered by a two-month-old unkempt beard. His black turtleneck sweater barely covers his waist line as he attempts to smooth it out as he approaches the men.

"Welcome aboard the *Mona Lucia*."

"Thank you, Captain Mustavich. It's a pleasure to meet you again."

"Yes, yes, likewise," he says. Then suddenly, the captain realizes only two had boarded. "Where is Yuri?"

"Unfortunately, we had a run-in with the authorities earlier today. They made sure that Mr. Gustav would not be joining us from here on out," Zen replies.

"That's…that's very unfortunate," the captain says in a sad tone. "Is he dead?"

"Uh, yes," the professor coldly replies.

"Oh, no," Mustavich says, turning around and walking to the small circle window of the office.

"He was my cousin. My family will be devastated to hear of the news."

"My condolences, Captain," Zen responds. "He was a good man."

Zen turns slightly toward Hank and rolls his eyes slightly as if indicating he truly didn't believe his own words.

Hank just stares back at Zen with a bewildered look.

"Thank you, Professor."

Mustavich stands silently for a moment and then turns his attention back to Hank, clearly seeing that he is injured. "We have a doctor on board that can take a look at your injury. If you like," the captain offers.

"That would be great, Thank you," Hank says, trying to show some genuine gratitude.

The ship's doctor finishes with the dressing on Hank's shoulder.

"There, you should be good as new before too long," the doctor says. "Luckily, the bullet didn't go too far down. Very minimal damage."

"That's good," Hank replies. "Thanks, Doc."

Hank slowly puts on a white button-up shirt. Face wincing a little over the strain of his injury.

The doctor proceeds to clean the office as Zen gestures to Hank to follow him out. As they walk on the deck of the ship, a scowl comes over his face.

"So, how is the shoulder?" Zen asks.

"Oh, it'll be fine," Hank replies.

"Are you well enough to take care of a task?"

"I don't know. What's the task?"

"Unfinished business," Zen says as the scowl remains on his face.

"What would that be?" Hank replies with a hint of confusion.

"Dr. Irvine," Zen answers. "He has your armored chest plate in his possession. We'll need that back. Also, the coward turned us in before the objective was met."

"I thought I was the objective you we're trying to achieve?"

"No, but you are very essential to the plan. A plan that Irvine nearly fouled single-handedly."

"What do you want me to do?"

"I want Irvine to pay!" Zen answers as he hits the ship's railing with his fist.

CHAPTER 40

The sun shines brilliantly through the stained glass windows of Berthel Church. It was a rarity that the sun would be so bright on a Sunday morning, especially during church service. One could almost sense the immediate lift in the congregation's spirits as the members seem to sing louder than normal over the selection of hymns for the service.

Dustin sits on the second row, listening to Pastor Phillips sermon on life verses. The pastor preaches on those certain Bible verses that resonate uniquely on individuals. Most Christians have that particular verse that speaks to them, giving them strength, comfort, and hope. Other verses, though, give them direction. For Dustin, he always felt that the verse from Matthew 4:19 spoke to him. "Come, follow Me," Jesus said, "and I will make you fisher of men."

It's a verse that brought hesitation to Dustin.

"How far am I to go for Him?" he asks himself.

The situation with Ginger and Hank breaks into his thinking and seems to throw him off track. A battle begins to wage in his mind. At times when he would become focused on God and his plans, something would always intervene and send his mind off in another tangent. Now, his mind races back and forth between Ginger and Hank.

Trying to make sense of their interaction and correlation seems a little overwhelming. The connection between the three makes his stomach turn.

Oh, if they only knew, he thinks to himself.

As the pastor ends his sermon and begins the invitation, Dustin makes his way to the back. He scans the congregation for Cameron and his mom. He locates the regular crew of classmates, Kevin, Abbey, and Grace, but Cameron cannot be found.

The church service ends and the congregation eventually filters out of the church. Carol Hobbs makes a point to stay behind and thank Pastor Phillips for his prayers and for coming by the hospital while Arnie was admitted.

"It's no problem at all, Carol," Philllips says. "By the way, where is he this morning?"

"Oh, he had to go in this morning," Carol answers. "There was a murder last night."

"Oh really?"

"Yes, it's horrible. Dr. Irvine, the one who was tied in with this whole Tankroid mess, was found dead this morning. What makes it even worse, he was in protective custody."

Pastor Phillips's face turns white in response to the news.

"I guess that Tankroid just ripped through the place, taking out the guards with ease. I just hope someone will stop him."

"Right, he needs to be stopped," the pastor says as he looks over the sanctuary where he sees Dustin engaging in a lighthearted conversation with a couple of teenagers from his Bible study class.

"Have any of you seen Cameron lately?" Dustin asks.

"Uh, no. I haven't seen or heard from him in days," Abbey replies.

"I know he's pretty hung up on that chick," Kevin adds.

"She's not a chick, Kevin. Her name is Jayden," Abbey says.

"Anyway, I think he's kinda sore that he hasn't gotten much support from us," Kevin states.

"What do you mean?" Dustin asks.

"Oh, you know. He's trying to help out this girl who is basically a lost cause," Kevin says.

"Nice, Kevin," Abbey replies. "If memory serves, you were a lost cause too at one point."

"Well…"

"What do you mean, 'a lost cause'?" Dustin enquires.

"She's just a bad seed. Knows nothing but being bad."

"But Cameron sees something else in her, right?"

"Yeah, I guess. He's a sucker for hard luck cases, I guess," Kevin replies.

"I was really hoping he would be here today, I better go by and see him later," Dustin states.

"Well, good luck with that," Kevin says, his eyes popping wide open, a gesture of it being a difficult task.

"Thanks for your support," Dustin says with a sarcastic smile.

"Here to serve!" Kevin replies with a smile.

"Oh whatever," Dustin responds, trying to mask his concern for Jayden and Cameron. He gives them a smirky smile, and says, "See you all on Wednesday."

Dustin looks up from his classmates to see Pastor Phillips approaching the group with a seemingly forced smile on his face.

"How are you all doing?"

"Pretty well," Abbey replies.

"That's good," the pastor responds. "Sorry to interrupt, but I need to steel Dustin for a moment."

"No problem," a couple of the kids say at the same time.

"Jinx! Buy me a soda!" they both say in unison.

"Nice," Dustin replies with a smile. "See you guys later." He waves good-bye at them as he follows Pastor Phillips to his office.

"What's wrong?" Dustin asks as the pastor unlocks his office door.

"It's bad."

"Like, making the news, bad?"

"Afraid so," Phillips replies as he enters his office and switches on the television. "Dustin, could you shut the door? I don't want anyone to hear the news reports."

"Sure," Dustin complies, closing the door behind him.

The picture came into focus as the BBC news reporter shows up on the screen.

Dustin feels cold chills run up and down his spine as he hears the news update. Showing the picture of Doctor Irvine in the corner of the screen, Dustin's mouth drops open.

"Holy cow! He was there that night I first encountered Tankroid." Dustin says. "He slipped out pretty quickly once I showed up."

"Yes, evidently he went to the authorities and spoke to Detective Hobbs," Phillips replies.

"So you didn't say anything to Mr. Hobbs about our situation?" Dustin asks.

"No," the pastor answers, but the look on his face indicated otherwise. "But he did stop by last week, right after your attack. He was starting to put the pieces together in his head."

"Does he know?" Dustin questions, feeling a little ill that someone had figured out his alter ego.

"He might," the pastor replies.

"Should I be concerned?"

Pastor Phillips opens his mouth to answer his last question when the news update from the television stops him.

"Our producers here at the BBC are expressing their concerns over our very own, Ginger Nevine. We have not heard from her nor can she be contacted. With her connection to Hank Jamerson and his alter ego 'Tankroid,' we fear the worst for her," the female reporter states.

"What?" Dustin says as he approaches the television. "What have I done?"

"Dustin, you didn't do anything."

"I should have protected her! I left her vulnerable!"

Dustin holds his hand to his mouth in disbelief.

"Any ideas?" Phillips asks.

"Let me grab my backpack. Do you mind going with me to her flat?"

"No, not at all," Phillips replies as he picks up the phone to tell his wife that he won't be home for a while.

They reached the neighborhood where Ginger's flat is located. Three squad cars are parked out in front of the apartment building. Slowly they walk up to the front door where an officer stands guard.

"Do you live here?" the cop asks Dustin.

"No, sir, I'm a friend of Ginger Nevine."

"Sorry, lad, but she's not here."

"I know, I was just hoping I could find something that might help me find out where she is."

"We have our top men on the case, young man. Go on home," the officer says.

"But—" Dustin replies but he is interrupted by a familiar voice.

"It's all right, Officer Parker. Let the young man in."

Dustin turns around to see Detective Hobbs following slowly up the steps behind him, still struggling with the use of his cane.

"Yes, sir," Officer Parker replies.

"Thank you, Arnie," Phillips said, looking back at him.

The three enter the building and proceed up one flight of stairs to Ginger's flat. Two officers are in the apartment dusting for fingerprints and searching for any other evidence they could find.

Dustin feels a little lightheaded thinking about the sheer terror Ginger must have been in when Tankroid kidnapped her. He prays quietly to himself that she is okay.

"So, now he's committed murder," Hobbs says of Tankroid.

Dustin shook his head no in disbelief.

"I don't understand. Believe me, I probably dislike Hank Jamerson more than anyone in this city. But I also know him well enough to know that he wouldn't kill someone in cold blood."

"Dustin, we have surveillance video of him entering the safe haven where Irvine was being kept," Hobbs explains.

"I'm not saying he didn't do it. I'm just saying that he must have done it against his will."

"What do you mean?" Hobbs questions.

"He's gotta be under control or something," Dustin says, carefully choosing his words to protect the information he had as well as his appearance when he discovered the controlling device the professor uses to control Hank.

"Well, whatever the case may be, we need to stop him," Hobbs says. Looking a little skeptical at Dustin, Hobbs asks, "So, what are you looking for?"

"I don't know yet. Can I look around?" Dustin asks.

Pausing for a moment, Detective Hobbs shakes his head yes. "Yeah, go ahead and look around."

Dustin slowly walks around the apartment, scanning over it until he reaches her bedroom. Standing there watching him, Hobbs leans into Phillips and whispers, "Trustworthy?"

Phillips just nods his head, "Yes."

Moments later, Dustin steps out of the bedroom, hands shoved in his pockets.

"Did you find anything?" Phillips asks.

"No. Everything seems to be in place," Dustin answers.

"You're right. There's no sign of struggle anywhere," Hobbs reports.

"Yeah, that kinda concerns me," Dustin answers as he fears that she might have gone willingly with him. Wondering what Ginger's mindset might be left Dustin questioning if he might be too emotionally invested into their relationship to be effective at all.

CHAPTER 41

On the second deck of the cargo ship, in a small cabin, Ginger sits on the bed looking at Hank as he stands leaning against the wall. He looks completely deflated from his normal cocky posture.

"I don't understand, Hank. How could you?" she asks through swollen red eyes.

"I didn't have control. I was forced to. You have to believe me," Hank replies. "That infernal device of Zen's makes me do whatever he desires me to do."

Ginger looks at her one-time hero in utter disbelief.

"But you said you went to them to get access to some kind of state of the art steroid formula."

"Yes, I did do that. I'll admit that, that was my fault. My intention was for more power, more strength. That VoLt thing really ticked me off with his statement to me that night that Jim was shot. He was so smug and arrogant with his power," Hank explains.

"What did he say to you?"

"Nothing, forget it."

"No, Hank. I want to know what he said to you that caused you to get all riled up at him."

"What, are you looking for a story to report?" Hank replies, knowing full well that the remark would sting Ginger.

"Nice, Hank," she replies as she rolls her eyes at him in disgust.

Hank pauses for a second, looking down at the floor. The slam at Ginger's expense didn't go over as well as he planned. She continues to stare at him as she could see the battle inside him as he comes to grips with his anger at VoLt.

"He said it was just a matter of time before everybody finds out the fraud I am."

"What? What does he know about you?"

"Beats me! That was the first time I ever met the creep."

"Do you think he knew about the steroids you took or the other stuff you were a part of?"

"How could he? There were only a small number of people who knew."

"Well, who were they?"

"I don't know, I guess Jake, Steve, and—" he pauses as he seems to dread repeating the last name. "And I guess the twerp."

"Twerp?"

"Yeah, you know, Dustin."

"Dustin knew about the steroids and stuff?" Ginger says as she pops up from the cot, quickly folding her arms, and breathing heavily.

"Yeah, you know, back in college. He never told you?" Hank asks surprisingly.

"No."

"Wow. I guess I had him pegged wrong," Hank replies with a seemingly new respect to Dustin.

"I can't believe he didn't tell me."

"Well, he did say that it would only be a matter of time before you would find out."

Hank raises an eyebrow as if he tries to make a connection with Dustin and his first encounter with VoLt. But the intense brain activity seems to be too much for Hank as he quickly dismisses the train of thought by quickly shaking his head.

"Whatever."

Ginger raises her eyebrow and glares at Hank. "You could never stand just being one of the guys on the team. You had to be the *man*, had to be the best. Now that egotistical thirst has landed us both in this predicament."

"I know, I know," Hank says as he put his hand over his eyes, as if hiding the tears that were forming. "I don't know what to do."

"Why am I here? Did you want me here?"

"No, I wanted you as far away as you could be, but Zen forced me to kidnap you and bring you here."

"Why?"

"Bait," he said in an embarrassed tone.

"Bait, bait for what?"

"VoLt," he answers.

"Why would you two intentionally lure VoLt here?"

"This is Zen's idea."

"Are you planning on killing him?"

"I don't know what the plan is."

"What about me? Are you going to kill me too?" she asks as the creases stretched across her forehead and brow.

"I…uh…I—" Hank pauses, suddenly aware of Ginger's potential doom. "I will not let that happen! I will let him know who is more powerful," Hank says in a conceited tone that started to resurface.

"How can you? You just said he had complete control over you!"

"Well, I won't let that happen," Hank answers.

He gazes out the small circular window in her cabin and a smirk comes to his face.

"Hey, I'm Hank 'The Tank'! Nobody can stop me!"

The look of despair quickly turns into a look of disgust as she reacts to his cocky tone.

"See, you have no control whatsoever!" Ginger shouts. "We're done!"

"Whatever," Hank replies as he stomps out of the cabin. "I'm outta here!" he yells as he locks the door behind him.

CHAPTER 42

Back at the Berthel Church, in his quarters, Dustin reaches inside the hidden doorway and takes the cloak off the hook. Nearly quivering in fear, Dustin gets undressed and puts on the black running shorts. Throwing on the cloak, he kneels down at his bed and begins to mediate in prayer.

His knuckles turn white as he grips his hands together. His heart races as he rocks back and forth slightly on his knees. Beads of sweat begin to form on his bare back beneath the heavy black wool cloak as the fabrics slightly itches his skin. He breathes through both his mouth and nose in an attempt to take in as much oxygen as he can. Then he finally softly mutters, "In your name I pray. Amen."

He stands up and stretches his arms up to where they almost touch the ceiling, then turns side to side in an attempt to stretch his abdomen as much as he can. Dustin realizes that he is not at a hundred percent, but he knows he can't wait until he is. Ginger is in trouble, and he seems to be her only hope.

Pastor Phillips sits in his office, praying himself. Finishing his prayer, he swivels his chair around to look out his stained glass window. The image was that of Christ praying on the rock just before the Roman soldiers took him away after Judas betrayed him with a kiss. He sits there studying the image like he had done many times before.

Suddenly there was a knock at the door. Pastor Phillips spins around and answers, "Come in."

The door opens and Detective Hobbs steps in. "Hello, Reverend."

"Oh, hey, Arnie," Phillips answers in a tone that indicates he wasn't expecting it to be Hobbs. "How are you feeling?"

"I'm improving, thanks," Hobbs answers. He leans slightly against the door to give his arm a chance to rest from supporting himself with the cane.

"Any updates?" Phillips asks.

"Funny, I was going to ask you the same thing."

Feeling a little uneasy at the question, he says, "No offense, Arnie, but I'm feeling a bit like Judas. I don't want to sacrifice the trust Dustin has in me."

"I understand, but I mean him no harm."

Reluctantly, Phillips stands up and smoothens out his shirt. "Let me go check on him."

"I'll wait here," Arnie said.

"Thanks," the pastor replies, knowing it is a respectful gesture on the detective's part, trying to reassure the trust they need to have for each other. Phillips reaches Dustin's quarters and knocks on his door.

"Dustin, are you in there?"

There is no answer. Taking a deep breath, he knocks again and asks, "Dustin?"

This time he opens the door and takes a peek inside. Dustin is gone, and the pastor could tell by how the dresser wasn't flush against the wall that VoLt was at work.

He closes the door behind him and heads back to his office.

Arnie stands in the pastor's office staring at the same stain glass window of Jesus praying as the pastor comes back in.

"I'm sorry, Arn, but…"

"He's at work?"

"Uh, yeah, it looks that way," the pastor says in an embarrassed tone.

"Very well. Now I know I need to be at the ready, just in case," Hobbs states. "Well, if you can excuse me."

"Sure," Pastor Phillips says as he steps back from the door, allowing Hobbs to exit.

"Oh, Arnie?"

"Yes, sir?" Hobbs stops as he turns around to face the pastor.

"Thanks for understanding."

"Thank you for your cooperation."

CHAPTER 43

VoLt runs along the subway corridor. He wants to start his search near her apartment, but realizes he has to be extra cautious not to be seen. VoLt estimates that he has to be close. Locating a sewer tunnel, he heads down the dark vein until he spots a manhole cover where he can escape. Using his strength, he manages to pop the cover loose, slowly lifting it up to make sure the coast is clear.

 The poorly lit street makes the conditions perfect for VoLt to climb out undetected. Once on street level, he checks to make sure he is still safe. Placing the manhole cover back in place, he looks for a rooftop that would be easily accessible. He spots a building, again poorly lit, that would suffice. Carefully climbing the fire escape, he reaches the rooftop. He is about two blocks away from Ginger's apartment. VoLt hopes he is close enough to pick up the trail. Reaching into his cloak's pocket, he pulls out a t-shirt of Ginger's that he manages to sneak out of her apartment earlier that day. Holding the shirt to his nose, he takes a big sniff. The scent is definitely hers. It's almost intoxicating to him. The scent of the girl he had grown to care so much about. The one he has always cared about. He wonders if his own scent is as enticing to her. Knowing the answer deep down, he presses on.

Instead of placing the shirt back in his pocket, he carefully laid it on the ground. Taking a step back, he searches the air for a similar scent. Testing all sides of the rooftop, he has difficulty finding it. On his second trip around the roof, he picks up on something. He stands still and sniffs again. On the southeast corner, he picks up on a possible trail. He descends down to the street level and hides behind a van as a car whizzes down the street. He then crosses the street to a building down a ways that he hopes will be in line with the trail.

A sense of comfort comes over him as he realizes that he doesn't appear to be hindered by his previous injuries as he climbs up and down the buildings with relative ease. Once he reaches the second rooftop, the scent is more defined. It's definitely Ginger's. He proceeds down the trail, leaping and dashing on buildings and through alleys as the trail leads him toward the Port of London.

Doubts begin to cloud VoLt's current location. He tries to understand why Zen would be at this cargo ship and questions if he had been following the right trail all along. It would make sense to him if he is wrong, since nothing has really gone to plan since Ginger resurfaced in his life.

VoLt hides behind a stack of cargo crates as he surveys the ship. The trail is still strong with his senses. The ship's markings indicated that its home port was Pakistan, which was Mr. Gustav's nationality. His gut tells him to continue to investigate as he carefully begins planning his way onto the ship. With his eyes, he follows the loading ramp to the ship's deck where he clearly sees someone standing guard, holding a rifle.

Well, that's a red flag, VoLt thinks to himself. The doubts start to subside as he realizes something questionable is at least going on somewhere on this ship.

As he scans the freightliner for other crewmembers, he hears the ship's crane start up. Soon he sees the crane's hoist begin to swing around to the shipping docks. VoLt watches as the large yellow metal arm comes to a complete stop as the hoist lowers. He watches as a crewmember on the docks waves his arm to the crane operator communicating to continue with the hook's decent. Standing on top of four crates tied together, the man retrieves the hook. He pulls it down until he has enough slack in the chain to hook up the cargo.

The crew hand securely fastens the cargo, double checking the straps holding the crates together. Then he proceeds to cross over to the next set of crates to be transported aboard. Each crate is approximately seven feet by seven feet in size, with each bundle being fourteen feet on each side of the lift. VoLt finds his opportunity to board. Using the shadows of the night for his cover, he leaps and grabs the straps of the cargo.

The crane whines as it lifts the cargo up, nearly seventy feet. The hoist swings back around and slowly lowers the shipment into the hull of the ship. Holding on to the outside of the crates, VoLt holds his breath, praying he will not be seen. He only sees the two ship hands in charge of the cargo loading. He figures this is his best way to board the ship undetected.

The hull is dark except for the light coming from the night sky and the few lights on deck. The crates finally touch ground as VoLt doesn't move until the mechanized hook releases and begins its accent. Carefully, he searches for a way out of the black pit he now finds himself in.

Ginger lies on the bare cot, looking at the ceiling, her eyes still red and slightly swollen from a recent period of crying. She has been locked alone in the room for nearly six hours without any kind of contact from anybody. Hearing the crane's engine start up, she sits up and walks over to look out her cabin's circle window as it begins to load crate after crate.

Staring at the door, she walks over to it and attempts to turn the knob. It's still locked. Letting out a disappointed sigh, she places her ear to the door, seemingly trying to hear anything on the other side of it. Hearing nothing, her shoulders drop as she walks back to her cot, defeated. She flops herself down and begins sobbing into the stale musty mattress. A few moments pass when a soft knock comes from the door. Ginger sits up and waits for whoever it is to enter, but instead, it appears someone is trying to open it without the key.

A surprised look comes over her face as she hears another knock on it lightly.

Cautiously, Ginger approaches the door and answers in a normal tone, "Hello?"

"Ginger, is that you?" asks a low, rumbly voice which Ginger did not recognize.

"Yes. Hank, is that you?"

There is a long pause, then the voice says, "Stand back from the door."

Ginger barely clears the door when it pops open as Ginger witnesses the creature VoLt thrust his way in by use of his shoulder. Quickly entering the room, he turns around and closes the door behind him.

VoLt turns back around to face Ginger, who stands in fear. "Are you okay?"

Shaking her head yes in a nervous manner, Ginger seems desperate to find the words to answer.

"Do you know how many are on the ship?" VoLt asks.

"I don't know for sure, I think maybe thirty," she answers with large eyes, leaving her mouth gaped open in awe.

"Okay," VoLt answers. "Is Zen on the ship?"

"Zen?"

"Yes, Professor Zen. The person your boyfriend broke out of jail last week," VoLt answers with a noticeable bit of agitation on his voice.

"He…he might be," Ginger replies as she looks up to the left, trying to recall who she has encountered on the ship.

"But Hank is here, right?" he asks.

"Yes, I think he's still here."

"Okay, first we need to get you out of here," VoLt growls.

He turns toward the door, but Ginger asks him a question that stops him in his tracks.

"What are you going to do to him?"

"What?" VoLt asks, refusing to turn around and look at her.

"What are you going to do to Hank?"

"He needs to be stopped," VoLt growls.

"Are you going to kill him?" she asks, fearing his answer.

VoLt is insulted by the question. It's not in his nature to kill anyone. But he does need to stop him regardless.

"He killed Dr. Irvine two nights ago."

"But he didn't have a choice," she states, pleading for his life.

"What do you mean?" VoLt asks as he turns around to face her.

"He said that some device has control over him. That he has to do whatever he's ordered to do."

VoLt had already assumed that Hank was under some kind of control, Ginger just happened to confirm it.

"Who has the device?"

"Professor Zen, I think?"

"Still, he has to be accountable for his actions… all of them," VoLt states in a tone that indicated that Hank is guilty of several wrongs.

"I know, I know…I just don't want to see him hurt," she says as she sits back down on the bed.

"But what about all the pain he's put you through? All the lies, the acts of selfishness? When are you going to have enough?" he asks.

"I am done, but still, I don't want to see him hurt."

VoLt stands there watching her as she weeps. He had seen this many times before. Dustin never understood why Ginger would always place herself in a situation where she could get hurt.

He'd warn her numerous times during their years together of the potential pain of her risks. She would always make herself vulnerable to heartbreaks from guys who only wanted what she wasn't offering, only to lose those guys who would find it from someone else.

Ginger would also leave herself susceptible to other girls who would attack her for going past her known social boundaries. It pained Dustin to see Ginger wind up hurt time after time. He would try to convince her to play it safe in many aspects of life, but her inner desire pushed her to reach for what was normally out of her reach.

Dustin finally began to realize that his own insecurities kept him from trying to achieve goals or overcome obstacles of his own. Those were the same insecurities that he realized he had been pushing on Ginger all this time. He thought he was protecting her, but now he realized that he had been hindering her all the way.

No wonder she went to college looking for excitement. Dustin has been holding her back unknowingly all along. Despite the fact that he was her spiritual safety net, it still pained him to see her hurt. But every time he witnessed a failure of Ginger's, it only refueled his cautious stance. A stance that he could not bear to watch anymore.

"Ginger, listen to me. I need you to go to the police station and ask for Detective Hobbs. Only speak to him. Once you find him, bring him back here," VoLt requests. "Do you understand?"

"Yes, but how do I get out of here?" She asks.

"Follow me," VoLt replies as he slowly opens the door and checks the deck for any shipmates. "We'll have to move quickly!"

Moments later, VoLt watches Ginger scamper down the ramp to the dock. She did her best to run as light-footed as she could, and as fast as she could. He has a brief flashback of her when they were kids. Visions of them running through the neighborhoods playing hide and seek replays in his mind. It was a far cry from the situation they found themselves in now.

VoLt waits until she is out of sight. Then he turns his attention back to the decks of the cargo ship. His impending battle waits for him somewhere, not too far away.

CHAPTER 44

Hank sits in a chair in the corner of the captain's quarters. He looks deflated, a far cry from the arrogant poise that he seemed to carry everywhere he went. His latest assignment had taken away nearly everything that he had worked for or had been given to him. Hank rubs his forehead in a possible attempt to rub the pain away or jump start his brain, seemingly hoping to find a solution to his current predicament.

"What's wrong, my boy?" Zen asks, looking up from the captain's desk that he and the captain lean over as a new route is plotted out for their journey.

"Nothing. Why you ask?" Hank answers back in a sarcastic tone.

"Don't worry about it. Irvine had it coming to him. Plain and simple," Zen stated coldly over the business decision to end their relationship with him.

"Then why didn't you take care of it yourself?" Hank asks with a stern look on his face.

"Well—"

"Because you couldn't do it yourself, that's why!" Jamerson shouts, answering his own question before the professor could attempt to reply himself.

"Careful, boy. Don't bite the hand that feeds you."

"How about I just rip your head off right now!" Hank yells as he shoots up to his feet and begins to charge Zen.

The professor stands frozen as Hank quickly approaches, but when Captain Mustavich pulls a pistol from his side, Hank comes to a quick stop.

"Don't do it, lad," the captain says as he points the gun at Hank. "He's too valuable to us."

Hank stands there glaring at the gun then turning his eyes on the professor who stood there with a smirk on his face. Then Zen raises an eyebrow in an attempt to dare Hank to continue his charge. Realizing the deck is stacked against him, he concedes in defeat and waves both arms down in Zen's direction.

"Whatever," Hank says as he looks at the captain with noticeable agitation. "I just want out of this."

"But this is what you wanted, isn't it?"

"What?"

"Yes, you wanted unmatched power. You were already tops in your league, but then you met the creature, and you realized he was more powerful than you. Plus, he rubbed you the wrong way. You were willing to do anything to acquire it. Please, stop me if I'm wrong," Zen states.

"I didn't expect to be your slave," Hank says simply as he turns to look out the dark window.

"There are always sacrifices with achievements."

VoLt carefully makes his way to the deck near the cargo hold. The ship is dimly lit, but his animal-like vision goes unaffected by the darkness. Sneaking around, he peers in each window hoping to locate either Zen or Hank. As VoLt makes it down to the deck along the ship's starboard side, he hears a gasp coming about twenty feet in front of him.

VoLt looks up to see a ship hand standing still, staring back at him. The whites of his widened eyes and gaped mouth indicates his startled surprise. Frantically trying to pull the rifle from his side, VoLt leaps through the air and knocks the assailant on his back. Just as the ship hand falls to the ground, the gun lets off a shot.

VoLt growls, "So much for the surprise attack."

Glaring at the ship hand, he grabs the rifle and flings it over the side of the boat and into the cold dark water. Then he grabs the terrified man and brings him to his face.

"Go!" VoLt barks.

With that, he releases him as the man didn't waste much time in following the beast's order. By now, VoLt can hear the commotion of several men heading in his direction. If they are all armed like this man, he realizes this might be a short battle.

"Give me strength!" VoLt prays as he begins charging down the deck, lowering his shoulder as if he was a football player anticipating a collision with an opponent. One door opens in front of him as a seasoned ship mate begins to step out, rifle in hand. Knowing that he has a split second advantage over the crewmember, VoLt lowers his head and rams the man in the chest just as he came into view.

"Ugh!" the crewmember yells in obvious pain and surprise as he falls back into the cabin.

VoLt grabs the pistol by the end of the barrel, and spinning around, he flings it into the water. Now the footsteps of other members can be heard hitting various floors of the ship. Knowing he has to pull out all stops, he realizes that just his sure presence would be enough to scare off most of the assailants.

He quickly has the opportunity to test out his theory as men start coming up the flight of stairs heading his direction. Looking up, he quickly counts four men as they cautiously try to see in the rapid approaching darkness. Waiting until the last second, VoLt lets out a roar that causes each man on the staircase to freeze in fear. The men quickly begin to retreat in panic as VoLt leaps over the staircase opening and the railing around it, then lands back down on the deck. Glancing up, he locates the ship's bridge. Planting hard with his left foot, he leaps with all his might. Soaring high through the air, he lands on the bridge's deck and proceeds to the ship's control room.

As VoLt charges for the bridge door, he roughly counts five men in the control room. Panic is apparent on their faces as they scramble to secure the door and to man their weapons. With a mighty thrust of his arms, the door breaks free of its hinges and falls on to three of the men as they fail to keep the creature out. Once inside, VoLt quickly sizes up the two remaining crewmembers as they both back up to their respective corners. One crewmember pulls his rifle up to aim at VoLt when he leaps through the air and tackles the assailant. Ripping the gun from his grasp, he hears the clicking of another rifle behind him. He spins around only to hear the rifle go off. VoLt hears the bullet whiz by him as it hits the other shipmate in the upper right chest. Glaring at the shaken crewmember with the rifle, VoLt lowers his shoulder and rams the gunman before he is able to send out another shot.

Anger begins to consume VoLt as he grabs the shooter by the throat and lifts him to his face.

"Where's the captain?" VoLt asks in a low, mean growl.

"He…he's…he's not here," the man answers as he gasps for air.

VoLt turns his attention back to the other crewmember who is able to get to his feet after having the door knock him down from VoLt's initial entrance. Backing against the controls that ran along the front window, the shipmate slowly brings up a gun, pointing it at VoLt. The young man is shaking as VoLt stares him down.

"Think about that first," VoLt says as he delivers a frightening frown at the assailant.

The shipmate's hand shakes wildly as his wide eyes stares down the creature. Displaying his gritted teeth, the young man pulls the trigger just as VoLt leaps through the air and tackles the assailant. The bullet misses VoLt but it goes through the creature's woolen cloak.

VoLt lands on top of the shipmate's chest as he glares down at the young man's eyes. There is no glow, no evil, just pure fear for his life. Taking advantage of his terrified state, VoLt leans down close to the man's face.

"Stay!" he roars.

The shipmate nods his head and nervously agrees.

"Good boy," VoLt replies.

Slowly, and eerily, he turns to face the other crewmembers as they attempt to get to their feet.

"As for you…" VoLt said as he begins to approach the crew hands.

They both drop to their knees, bowing down in fear of the creature.

"Please, don't hurt me!" One man cries as he crawls into a ball. "I'll stay here too. I won't do anything against you!"

"Deal!" VoLt growls.

He glares at the other, "And you?"

"I stay, I stay!" he says in broken English.

VoLt stands over the men as he glances over the window. To his surprise, he finds Tankroid standing next to Zen, square in the middle of the main deck. Both adversaries stare back at VoLt as their glares pierce the dark London night.

VoLt exits the bridge of the ship and walks around on the front deck of the bridge that looks down on the main deck of the ship.

"Are you ready for round two, my boy?" Zen yells out.

You mean round three, Volt thinks to himself.

VoLt paces back and forth on the upper deck as he stretches out his hands and then brings them in, making fists, preparing himself for battle. Feeling his heart beat out of his chest, he grabs the rail and leaps over, dropping onto the deck. Landing on all fours, he stares down his adversaries while mentally taking a quick assessment of his body. Nearly no pain to which he attributes to the rush of adrenaline that is flowing through his body.

Tankroid growls as electrical streams can be seen shooting around the armored chest plate he wears. Zen whispers something in Tankroid's ear, undetectable by VoLt. Surveying the area around him, he's suddenly reminded of the huge opening in the deck that leads down to the cargo area in the ship's belly. Looking back up, he sees Tankroid slowly approach with an evil, mean stare.

"How long are you going to be his trained dog?" VoLt yells.

Surprisingly, Tankroid doesn't respond. He just keeps his fixated glare on VoLt, then suddenly, Tankroid charges. VoLt readies himself as he makes a mental note to avoid contact with the metal chest plate the dog-like creature wore. Tankroid sails through the air, claws out, aiming for VoLt. Grabbing his enemy by the shoulders and grinding his teeth, VoLt digs his own claws into Tankroid and flings the mighty beast over his head.

Tankroid roars in pain and frustration as he lands hard in the concrete deck on his side. As the creature attempts to stand up, VoLt attacks with fury, delivering powerful blow after blow with his right fist to Tankroid's jaw. VoLt takes a step back, giving the creature a quick assessment and planning his next maneuver. Tankroid staggers to his feet as an irate Professor Zen can be heard yelling in disgust.

"Tear him apart!"

With that order comes a sudden jolt of electrical shocks to Tankroid's chest plate.

VoLt glances over to Zen as he watches him man the controls of the remote device. Tankroid seizes the opportunity and attacks VoLt. Wrapping him up and tackling him to the ground, Tankroid squeezes VoLt tightly against his chest as electricity shoots out, shocking VoLt relentlessly.

VoLt grimaces in pain as his muscles and limbs lock up. Tankroid keeps a tight grip on him as he rolls him over. Straddling his opponent, and with enormous strength, he power lifts himself up with his legs, all the while bear hugging VoLt.

A loud roar is released from Tankroid as he violently throws VoLt onto the hard concrete ship deck. Tankroid stands over VoLt, electric shockwaves rippling over his metal chest plate.

"Finish him!" Professor Zen commands.

Tankroid glances over to Zen as he receives his orders and delivers an evil glare.

"I said, finish him!" Zen re-orders as he holds up the remote control device, slightly waving it with his hand.

Following his orders, Tankroid bends down and grabs VoLt by the back of his mane and pulls him up to his knees. A weakened VoLt looks up at his adversary, trying to muster the strength to defend himself.

"Your time's up, mutt!" Tankroid growls.

Tankroid cocks his arm back to deliver a devastating punch when VoLt mutters a question.

"Th….then what…happens?"

Tankroid paused, arm still cocked.

"What?"

"What becomes of you? A lifetime as a trained pet?"

Agitated, Tankroid grabs VoLt and lifts him up to his feet.

"What's it to you?"

VoLt lets his head fall back, and then he rapidly thrusts his head forward, head butting Tankroid.

"Ugh!" Tankroid growls as he is forced to release his grip on VoLt and cover his eyes as if trying to shield from the sudden shock of pain to his forehead.

Seeing stars of his own, VoLt focuses his attention on Tankroid's head as he delivers a hard punch with his right to Tankroid's left jaw, then counters with a left to Tankroid's right jaw.

Tankroid staggers around leaving his unshielded back exposed. VoLt charges from behind and tackles Tankroid, forcing him to land hard on the surface as sparks of electricity shoot out from his chest plate. VoLt proceeds to jump to his feet and glances over to Zen.

The look of disgust is vividly apparent on the professor's face. Zen quickly mans the control device as a battered Tankroid is forced to quickly jump to his feet. Roaring in pain, he charges at VoLt.

VoLt quickly firms up his stance as the creature approaches. Tankroid charges with both arms in the air. Fist clutched together as if holding a sledgehammer, prepared to swing down with a thunderous blow. Just as he reaches striking distance, VoLt connects with a quick thunderous blow of his own against the metal chest of Tankroid. A fury of blue electric sparks erupts as streams of electricity shoot out, some making contact with Tankroid's body.

Tankroid staggers, thriving in pain, face grimacing as he tries to fight off the burning jolts. VoLt stands helplessly by as he watches the creature stagger close to the edge of the deep cargo hold. Then suddenly, Tankroid finds himself on the verge of falling into the black pit.

"Hank!" VoLt shouts out, surprised to find himself feeling concern for him, even for a split second. He even steps forward to be within arm's grasp if need be.

Tankroid reaches out for VoLt, but manages to grab him by the gold V medallion. Quickly, VoLt reaches up to grab Tankroid by the wrist that held the shiny metallic piece, but even VoLt's reflexes weren't fast enough as the aged old leather straps that held the medallion around his neck easily gives way.

Suddenly VoLt watches Tankroid fall into the cargo pit as he watches the glow of the medallion fade into the darkness fully clenched on Tankroid's grasp. Dustin instantly feels the unfortunate transformation of his body. Quickly, Dustin throws his black hood over his face in an attempt to conceal his identity.

"Success!" Zen yells.

Dustin cautiously peeks through his heavy hood as Zen begins strutting toward him.

"Finally! After years of waiting, planning, and… well…executing… I have the mighty power of VoLt nearly in my grasp."

Dustin's heart races as he begins to realize the dire situation of the moment. Zen comes to a stop roughly fifteen feet in front of Dustin, just where the ladder from the cargo hold starts its decent into the abyss.

"Go ahead, hide behind that hood of yours while you can. It'll be over shortly."

Zen looks down into the black hull beneath him.

"Are you still with me, my boy?" Zen shouts into the cargo hold.

Dustin could hear Tankroid growling.

"I'm not your boy!"

Zen rolls his eyes.

"Whatever. Just bring up the medallion."

There was an eerie, awkward long pause. A quick look of agitation comes over the professor's face.

"Bring it up now!"

With that, Zen again mans the controls as the creature can be heard grunting and growling as Tankroid begins to climb the ladder. Each second that passes, Dustin tries desperately to think of a way out of this predicament. Finally, Tankroid begins to appear as he reaches the top of the hull to the ship's deck. Gingerly, the creature steps onto the deck, glancing first at Dustin and then glancing back to Zen.

"You want this?" Tankroid asks, holding the medallion in his paw in plain sight.

Zen stares at the creature cautiously, as if trying to understand the question.

With a quick sudden movement, Tankroid pulls back his arm in attempt to heave the medallion into the cold waters of the River Thames. Calmly and coolly, as if he anticipated his move, Zen pushes a control button that locks Tankroid in position with his arm pulled back. The creature grits his teeth as he couldn't ease the muscle lock of his body.

"Ah, ah, ah," Zen says as he waves his finger back and forth toward Tankroid. "We will be having none of that."

The professor walks smoothly over to the statue-like creature, appearing to savor every moment of his long enduring venture to finally hold the mysterious gold medallion in his grasp.

Dustin looks on in sheer disbelief at what's happening before him. His mind races as he tries desperately to think of his next move.

Zen studies the gold medallion in the creature's hand. The leather straps that are connected to the golden piece drape down from Tankroid's clutch. Zen reaches over and grabs the leather straps, then violently yanks the medallion from the beast's frozen grip.

Tankroid growls in pain as the golden piece slices open his paw as it is yanked from his hand.

"What are you going to do?" Dustin finally asks.

Looking annoyed to have the hooded figure address him, he slowly glances over his shoulder at Dustin.

"I'm going to show you want real power looks like."

With that response, Zen holds up the gold medallion to where he can see it dangle in front of him with his right arm. An evil smile comes over his face. Tying the old leather straps together again, he places the medallion around his neck as it rests on his expensive tailored white shirt. Then he bends down and places the remote control device down on the ground. Turning around to face Dustin and the immovable figure of Tankroid, he ceremoniously rips his shirt open as the buttons can be heard popping off. The gold metal medallion now rests on Zen's bare chest.

"At last! Victory is mine!"

But as soon as he shouts his triumph, the V-shaped medallion begins to burn against his chest. Zen grimaces in agony as he appears to try to power through the pain, perhaps thinking this is just part of the process. Instead, the medallion begins to become hotter and hotter. Finally, it becomes too painful for him as he yells in agony. He reaches up and pulls the medallion from his chest. Zen quickly discovers that the gold piece is also burning his hand as it comes in contact with it too.

Taking advantage of the opportunity, Dustin charges Zen, ramming him with all his might into Zen's back. Zen grunts in pain from the attack as they both fall to the floor. Dustin quickly looks around for the medallion and finds it lying on the deck next to Zen. Trying to get to his feet, Dustin suddenly feels the soreness in his ribs from the previous injury which didn't appear to be as healed in his normal state.

Grinding his teeth he scampers toward the V-shaped piece. Apparently aware of the situation, Zen quickly grabs the leather straps of the medallion and pulls it to him, all the while suffering in extreme pain.

"Not so fast," Zen groans.

Desperately looking for an advantage, Dustin finds himself looking at Tankroid, still in his statue-like state.

"Help me," the beast cries.

Dustin glances down and locates Zen's remote control device on the ground between him and the professor. With all the strength he can muster, he bolts for the control device. Zen, seemingly knowing Dustin's objective, moves toward the device also. The two get into reaching distance at the same time when Dustin delivers a blow to Zen's wounded chest. Zen stammers back in agony as Dustin grabs the remote control.

"Release me!" Tankroid yells.

Frantically, Dustin tries to determine which button would release him. Rapidly studying it, the red button catches his attention.

Hopefully, red means stop! Dustin thinks to himself.

Pressing it, he instantly witnesses Tankroid's body become free from its frozen state. The creature only takes a moment to catch his breath and then attacks Zen. Like a seasoned boxer, Tankroid delivers punch after punch to Zen's body. Tankroid seems to be having a field day as he finally is freed from his master. The creature easily manhandles the professor as Zen begins to beg for mercy, all the while holding onto the leather straps of the medallion for dear life.

"Please, stop," Zen pleads as he rolls on the ship's desk.

He holds his hands up in a sign of surrender.

"Why?" Tankroid asks between gritted teeth.

"I'll give you whatever you want."

Dustin could hardly believe his eyes and ears as he realizes that he and Hank are allies for the moment as they stand over Professor Zen. Dustin takes the moment to respond to Zen's bargain offer.

"You know what I want!" Dustin yells from under the hooded cloak that he has managed to stay hidden under, even during the previous struggle with Zen.

"I want the—" Dustin begins to finish his request when suddenly he witnesses Tankroid reach down, lift Zen up and throw him overboard, with the medallion still in his grasp.

"No!" Dustin yells as he finds himself running to the ship's side. Hearing Zen hit the water below, Dustin looks over the edge into the nearly pitch black water, trying to locate Zen. Suddenly, Dustin realizes that he is standing next to the man that he despised almost more than any one. The same man that took his best friend away from him, the same one that nearly took away his life just days ago, and now the same one who has just thrown away one of the most precious gifts he would ever receive.

"What have you done?" Dustin asks as he can feel the sudden rush of emotions flood his head.

"It needed to be done," the creature said as he looks into the same dark river.

Then Tankroid slowly turns and faces Dustin. Dustin cautiously begins to step back from the edge's railing. He finds himself still holding the remote control device. Anger flows through his veins as he holds it up in front of him, almost threatening the mighty beast.

Tankroid stands still, seemingly trying to determine Dustin's next move.

Suddenly, Dustin can hear numerous footsteps charge up the ship's boarding ramp. Knowing it is the authorities, he carefully moves around Tankroid and begins walking to the bow of the ship.

"What are you going to do?" Tankroid asks.

Dustin wasn't too sure himself. He wanted Hank to pay, he wanted Zen to pay, but vengeance for himself is not what VoLt is about. It is about aiding those who can't aid themselves and to even aid the wrongdoers in their grasp of evil.

"Hold it right there!" shouts a police officer as he points a pistol at Tankroid, all the while keeping an eye on Dustin.

Looking up, Dustin counts ten officers charging up the boarding ramp with Detective Hobbs following closely behind. As they approach the ship's deck, he finds Ginger following them with desperation on her face. Dustin holds up the device and quickly studies it again, biting his lip, he presses a blue button.

Dustin, along with twelve others, watch in amazement as Tankroid transforms bank into Hank Jamerson. Struggling to see from underneath his hood, Dustin watches Ginger's expression as she places her hand over her mouth in an attempt to control her emotions.

Glancing back to Hank, he sees Hank mouth a response in his direction.

"Thank you."

Slowly bending down, Dustin places the remote control device on the ship's deck. Standing back up, he glances over to Detective Hobbs.

Hobbs looks back at Dustin with an angry stare as if saying, "Don't do it!"

But without much thought, Dustin quickly spins around, throws off his cloak and jumps over the railing into the frigid waters below. All the while Dustin could hear Detective Hobbs and the other officers yell.

"No! Wait! Don't jump!"

Dustin did not fall gracefully into the river. His body and head hit with such force that his head snaps back as his jaw smacks the water. That, along with the stinging sensation of the icy cold water, nearly sent his body into shock. With all the strength he could muster, he swims to the edge of the ship and frantically begins looking for Zen. His teeth chatter rigorously as he scans the waters for him. Hope begins fleeting fast as beams of light from above start scanning the waters. Dustin then realizes that Zen is gone. Only thing he could do is get away too. Taking a deep breath, he goes under and tries to swim as fast and as far as he can.

Above, Detective Hobbs walks to the spot where Dustin leaped from the ship's deck, still with an aid of the cane. Carefully, he bends down and picks up the black woolen cloak. Holding it in front of him, he looks out over the water. Hobbs shakes his head back and forth in disbelief.

"Crazy kid."

Hobbs turns around to see Ginger embrace Jamerson as they place handcuffs on him.

"Let's get him out of here before the TV reporters get here," Hobbs orders.

"Right, sir," responds one of the officers.

"Ms. Nevine," Hobbs said as she tries to let Ginger know that she has to let Hank go.

"I'm so sorry, babe. So sorry," Hank mumbles as tears stream down his face.

"I know, I know," she answers as she reluctantly releases him.

The officers proceed to escort Jamerson across the deck, down the ramp and into a waiting police car.

Hobbs waddles his way over to Ginger as he keeps an eye on the ship's captain that had been watching from above as the scene played out.

"Thank you for getting that unwelcomed riff raff off my ship, Officer," Captain Mustavich says.

"Right," Hobbs answers with a cold steel look.

"Miss Nevine, let's go," Hobbs said, all the while keeping an eye on Mustavich.

Ginger stares out over the water, perhaps trying to determine the fate of the individual who jumped off the ship, or trying to determine her own fate. Either way, she didn't say a word. She just simply follows the detective's orders as he leads her away from the scene.

CHAPTER 45

On the river walkway that runs beside the Thames, sitting underneath one of numerous bridges that cross it, Dustin sits shivering in the cold air, soaking wet. He rocks back and forth in a cradled position, weeping.

"Forgive me, Lord. I have failed you." Tears are streaming down his face. "Please, forgive me."

He buries his face in his arms.

In the moments that pass in between the sounds of his own sniffling, he can hear a squeaky noise slowly approaching him. Cautiously, he lifts his head up to see what could be causing the noise. Squinting his eyes in the dark air, he slowly begins to make out a silhouette of an old man pushing an old squeaky shopping cart. Dustin doesn't move as he approaches, almost hoping to go undetected.

The old man with long, gray, dirty hair that cascades down from a dark-colored stocking cap stops right at Dustin's feet. The homeless man stands there studying him as his tongue rolls around his nearly toothless mouth.

"Son, you're gonna catch a death of a cold," the old man says as he begins riffling through his cart.

"It's okay, I deserve it."

"Now hush," the old man says as he continues to search with his hands that were wrapped in red cloth.

Dustin studies the red and green plaid shirted hobo as he digs through his stuff.

"Here, put this on," the old man orders.

The hobo threw a pair of old green sweatpants and a dingy brown sweater to Dustin. He can feel the sudden warmth that it would give him.

"I…I can't."

"Yes, you can. And you will"

"Are you sure?"

"That's what we're supposed to do. Help out each other."

The old man continues to rummage through his collection as Dustin puts on the sweatpants and sweater. He feels instantly better once he throws them on. He looks at the good Samaritan with sincere gratitude.

"Ah…there they are!" the old man proclaims.

He pulls out a pair of old sneakers and hands them over to Dustin. Taking them, he slides them on easily, since they were three sizes too big. Looking down at his new attire, guilt consumes him.

"I feel horrible for taking your clothes," Dustin says.

"They're not mine, they're yours," the old man replies, looking at Dustin with a sense of matter of fact.

"I don't know what to say."

"Don't need to say a thing. Just go back and fix what put you in this predicament."

"What?"

"Obviously, you've lost something important in your life. Why else would you be here, sopping wet, cold, and distraught."

Goosebumps run up his spine as he feels someone might be speaking through him.

"How do I fix it? How do I find it?" Dustin nervously asks.

"You'll have to figure that out for yourself."

The hobo begins putting things back in random order in his cart.

"A man doesn't truly know what he has until it's gone." The hobo pauses. He looks at his belongings in his shopping cart, but it appears to Dustin that he seems to be looking beyond his collection. "You'll darn near kill yourself trying to get it all back."

Dustin doesn't say a word. He just allows the words to sink in.

"You'll venture down paths you've never been. It'll take you to the ends of the earth. You'll be tested like you've never been tested. And you'll discover things about yourself you never knew."

The man starts to walk away, pushing the cart from behind. Glancing back at Dustin slightly, he parts with, "Godspeed, lad."

Dustin watches as the hobo vanishes into the darkness as the squeaky wheels of the cart start to fade out against the sound of the flowing river.

Still feeling the chill of the cold London air, Dustin begins the difficult replay of all of his decisions as of late. Did he handle the situation with Ginger correctly?

He knew that it has been consuming most of his life and thoughts since she reentered back into his life.

"I should have stayed focused on the kids in my class. Lord knows they have enough going on…"

Dustin stops himself in midsentence as one of the situations of a certain young man and young woman broke through his conscience like a wrecking ball. He realizes that any ability to save Jayden from her plight had just disappeared into the cold River Thames.

"Oh no, what have I done?" Dustin says to himself.

Responding as if a pistol had been shot to start a race, Dustin breaks into a sprint. Water splashes up from his feet as he rapidly runs through the puddles toward home.

CHAPTER 46

The chimes of Big Ben echo over the city. As Dustin closes in on Cameron's flat, he waits to count the chimes to see what time it could be, all the while trying to maintain his pace. Panting heavily in the oversized shoes and musty old clothes, he begins counting. One chime echoed. Dustin looks back in the direction that Big Ben resides, waiting for at least nine or ten more chimes, but nothing followed.

One? he thinks. *He's probably asleep by now.*

He reaches the modest apartment building and scans the second floor from the sidewalk below. Trying his best to recall the exact windows of Cameron's flat, he searches for any kind of light coming from his residence. Deciding to walk around toward the alley next to the building, he continues to stay focused on the second floor.

One window catches his attention as he can see light coming from it. The window opens to an old, dilapidated fire escape. The bottom ladder from the black rusted structure hung about two feet above Dustin's reach. Jumping up with all his might and stretching out as far as he could, he manages to miss the ladder. Landing on the ground, sharp pain shoots up his left side.

Dustin quickly grabs his ribs and he is instantly reminded of his recent injuries from the first encounter with the kronog, Tankroid. Gritting his teeth and still staying focused on the objective at hand, he looks for something he could use as a springboard that would enable him to reach the ladder. He can't find anything that would suffice.

Taking a deep breath, he gives himself about fifteen feet of acceleration distance in the alley that would hopefully allow him the momentum needed to reach the ladder. With the biggest burst of speed he could muster, he charges down the alley, leaping just feet in front to the ladder. Extending his arms, hands, and fingers, he grimaces as he sails through the air.

To his surprise, Dustin feels the dirty, rusty metal step bar with his hands as he clasps it with all his might. The fire escape clanks and rattles at his grasp. As his weight continues to swing forward, the ladder's latch that holds it in place gives way to Dustin's swaying body. The ladder suddenly drops straight down as intended by design, causing Dustin to experience the instant feeling of falling.

The ladder's descent comes to an abrupt stop which causes Dustin to lose his grip and fall flat on his back, knocking the wind out of him. As he gasps desperately for air, he suddenly sees his vision begin to turn black.

Dustin finally wakes up, still lying on the ground in the alley. His eyes begin to focus on an individual that stands over him. He becomes aware that the individual is speaking to him, but he has difficulty understanding what is being said to him. Fighting off intense pain in his back and left ribs, he tries to focus on the figure addressing him.

"I said, are you okay?" the individual asks.

"Uhhh," Dustin mutters.

"Do you need help?"

Despite his current situation, the question seemed rather loaded to him. Of course he needs help, but in what capacity is this individual referring to?

Managing to roll over on his right side, he tries to get a handle on his breathing.

"Dustin, what were you trying to do?" asks the voice.

With eyes wide open, almost bulging out of his sockets from the pressure built in his head, he begins focusing on the person.

"Cam?" he gasps out.

"Yeah," he paused. "Are you okay?"

Dustin manages to roll around and sits on his rear on the alley floor.

"Well, I was till I tried that stunt."

He reaches around with his right arm to his back in an attempt to ease the pain.

"Why are you here?" Cameron asks.

"To help you," Dustin answers.

A look of disbelief comes over Cameron as he tries to grapple with the aid that Dustin is capable to offering.

"Help with what? Being caught?"

"No. Jayden," Dustin replies. Still wincing from pain, embarrassment fills him as his attempt as a crime fighter fails in comparison to his alter ego.

"It's too late," Cameron answers in a deflated tone. "Why do you want to help now? It sounds like your lady friend is in quite a bit of trouble herself."

"She's fine," Dustin answers flatly.

Dustin is finally able to get to his feet where he can look Cameron in the eyes, all the while still nursing his injuries.

"Cam, I'm sorry. I let you down. And I know that I let Jayden down."

"It's like she said herself, she's a lost cause," Cameron says.

The fact that both Jayden and Kevin, from a previous conversation, refer to her as a "lost cause" made Dustin even more determined to aid her and help turn her life around, somehow.

Cameron turns around as if he intended to go back inside, leaving Dustin alone out in the cold.

"Cam, we can still help her," Dustin pleads.

Cameron stops, but he didn't turn around, he just simply asks, "How?"

"I don't know yet. But I'll do whatever I can. I promise."

Dustin could see Cameron's stone face begin to break.

"Cam, I know I failed. I failed a lot here of late. Just let me try to get back on track."

Cameron begins to speak through a quivering voice. "I thought he would show up somehow. You know, the way he showed up for me that one night, over a year ago."

Knowing who Cameron is referring to, he didn't respond.

"But I guess he's too busy these days too."

Cameron slowly turns around to look at a pitiful Dustin standing there in worn-out clothes covered in dirt and dampness.

"Well, maybe you should clean up first?"

"Yeah, you're right." Dustin replies, feeling the tension between them ease up a bit with the possibility of trust beginning to build back up.

CHAPTER 47

The next afternoon, Dustin is nursing a cold as he prepares a Bible study lesson. He knows he has to find Jayden. How he is going to do it still remained a mystery. He purposely avoids hearing or reading any news regarding Hank and the disappearance of Zen. Dustin even asked Pastor Phillips to keep any news regarding it to himself. He had to focus on Cameron and Jayden as well as the rest of his class. He had to admit to himself that his head has not been where it needed to be. Dustin knew he would have to be accountable for his lack of leadership to the group, and he had to prove it, especially to Cameron. As he continues to prepare for class, there is a knock on his door.

"Just a second," he replies, placing a bookmark in his Bible.

Expecting it to be the pastor, he opens the door. His eyes pop wide open when he sees Detective Hobbs standing there before him.

"Uh, good afternoon, sir," Dustin says.

His heart races as his mind runs wild with possibilities to the detective's sudden visit.

"Hello, Dustin. Did I catch you at a bad time?" Hobbs asks without a hint of emotion on his face.

"No…no… not at all. Just prepping for class."

There is an awkward moment of silence when Dustin's manners finally kick in.

"Oh, won't you come in?" Dustin asks.

He opens the door and gestures with his right arm the invitation to enter.

"Thanks," Hobbs responds.

The detective stops and smoothly looks around Dustin's living quarters. Raising his eyebrows lightly as he looks back at Dustin, he lifts up a brown grocery bag and hands it to Dustin.

Dustin slowly reaches out for it as he tries to figure out what would be in this brown worn out bag.

"Thought you might need this," Hobbs says as a small smile cracked his stone-like face.

Dustin peeks inside the bag. Shock and a bit of embarrassment comes over him as he recognizes the aged old black wool hooded cloak. His mouth drops open, but no words come out. He looks back up at Detective Hobbs. Dustin struggles with the reality that is sinking in.

"How...how did you know?" Dustin asks.

"Dustin, I'm a detective. I just had to connect the dots."

"Oh."

Dustin makes a face indicating he would have to be more careful, then he realizes that he might not have to worry about it anymore.

Dustin proceeds to pull the cloak out of the bag and holds it up. He's glad to have the sixty-five-year-old garment back in his possession. The musty scent smells like flowers to him.

"Did you find Professor Zen?" Dustin asks.

"Nope," Hobbs replies, following it with pursed lips.

Hobbs widens his stance, lets out a sigh of relief, and crosses his arms. A sign to Dustin that the tension in the room had eased up as they both were on the same page, no secrets.

"We had divers looking for his body for the past two days. No signs of him." Hobbs says.

Dustin turns and walks toward the window. Looking into nothingness as Zen's fate floods his mind.

"Do you think he's dead?"

"Probably. I understand that Hank Jamerson nearly beat him to death just before he threw him into the river."

"Yeah, it was pretty brutal."

"But hey, somehow you survived the fall and icy cold water."

"Yeah, barely."

Pausing for a moment, seemingly to know what else Dustin might be missing.

"Oh, and we did look for a particular shiny gold metal piece."

Dustin felt his ears perk up as he turns around to meet Hobbs face to face.

"And?"

"Sorry lad, no luck."

Dustin just nods his head up and down in regrettable understanding.

"Well, without that, VoLt is gone."

"Son, his heart still remains," Hobbs says as he reaches over and grabs Dustin's shoulder, squeezing it gently. He follows that with a pat on the back.

Dustin turns back around and looks out the window with a blank stare. Hobbs takes the opportunity to quietly step out and leave Dustin alone with his thoughts. Finally the realization of his failure resonates with his soul. A list of individuals flood his mind of people he had let down. Tim Warner entrusted him with the mantle of VoLt, Jessica Parsons had complete faith in him to carry out the calling. Pastor Phillips risked his character to defend him, and God had blessed him with these unique powers in an attempt to save so many souls. Now the realization of his own selfishness and ego had resulted in the enormous failure at his calling.

CHAPTER 48

The Bible study class wraps up with the students engaging in light hearted conversation. Many of the teenagers were unaware of Dustin's mental absentness over the past month or so. His general apology fell on deaf ears as they quietly and easily forgave him.

At the end of class, Cameron comes up to Dustin. "I think I have a lead on where Jayden is."

"Really, that's great! Where?"

"Well, I'm trying to sneak into the group through this kid I know."

"Cam, that sounds dangerous."

"I'll be fine. I'm not going to do anything, I'm trying to figure out where they are."

"Okay, but don't go to deep. They have ways of pulling you in."

"I know, I just wanted you to know…you know?"

Dustin could see how much this girl meant to Cameron. It was the same feeling that he had had for Ginger, and it nearly killed him.

"All right, just keep me informed."

"Will do," Cameron replies as he turns and leaves the classroom.

Leaving the classroom himself, Dustin is in the midst of shutting off the light and closing the door when he hears a familiar voice softly speak to him.

"How was your class tonight?"

Dustin turns around with an expressionless face.

"It went well, thanks."

Closing the door behind him, he feels his hands go cold and numb as he focuses on the individual in front of him. His stomach starts to turn. His heart races as he tries to put up his best defense.

"What have you been up to, Gin?"

Dustin clasps his teeth together tight in an attempt not to show any emotion.

"Really?" she asks sarcastically.

She raises an eyebrow, questioning his attitude.

Tension fills the air around them. A few awkward moments pass as they wait for the other to start the discussion.

"Are you okay?" Dustin asks reluctantly.

"What do you think?"

"I'm sorry, Ginger. I don't know what to think."

"Neither do I."

Again, a few moments of silence pass. Dustin proceeds to lean against one wall as Ginger mimics him as she leans against the wall across from him.

"I lost my job at the BBC because of all of it," Ginger says, rolling her head back looking at the white tile ceiling.

"Sorry."

"It's my fault. I should have known that his selfish greed would eventually be his downfall and that he would take everyone down around him. All in a pitiful attempt to get what he wanted."

"But yet you still feel something for him?"

"I feel frustration, stupidity, disappointment—"

"But you still feel something for him," Dustin interrupts.

"I don't know," she says, as she rolls her head along the wall and looks at Dustin. "What about us?" she asks.

"About us?" Dustin states. "Oh, we're fine." He pushes himself off the wall and stands firmly on his two feet. "We're just fine."

He didn't believe it, and he's pretty positive she didn't either.

Dustin escorts her to the church's main door as they do their best to exchange small talk. Knowing that this might be the last conversation he would have with her, he did his best to act as if they would still be in everyday contact, but he knew better.

"Well, I do have a lead on a reporter job in the US," she says as she reaches the door, looking back at Dustin for some kind of encouragement.

"Really? That's great." Trying his best to show support in their inevitable end.

"Yeah, but I don't know. I don't want to leave."

"Why not? It's a clean slate! A fresh new start," Dustin states.

Ginger's chin drops, her forehead wrinkles. She seemingly understands why the need for a "fresh start."

"Uh, yeah. A clean slate," Ginger says as tears start to build in her eyes.

Dustin realizes that Ginger knows that this was good-bye as well.

"Without a safety net and no fear," Dustin replies. "I hope you find what you're looking for, Ginger."

Shoving his hands in his pockets as if he's shivering from the sudden emptiness that is about to fill his heart.

"Like you said a couple of days ago, I just need to find me," Ginger said. "Wherever that might be."

He wants to hold her one last night, take in one more fragrance of her perfume. He can see the struggle in her eyes to do the same.

"Keep in touch?" she asks.

"Always."

Now tears were welling up in his eyes as she opens the door and steps out. Softly closing the door behind her, she looks at Dustin one last time and softly whispers, "Bye."

"Bye," he mouths to her without making a sound, watching as the door closes. He waves good-bye.

Lightheaded and numb, he turns and makes his way to his room. With each step, he knows that he would no longer hear or see Ginger again. He finally reaches his quarters where he collapses on his bed, consumed in heartbreak.

CHAPTER 49

In the following days, Dustin finds himself feeling some remorse for Hank's situation. Pastor Phillips tries to offer words of comfort in one of their weekly sessions.

"Hank could not control the monster inside him. His thirst of greed led to his ultimate demise," says the pastor. He continues as Dustin stares out the window. "We all have monsters inside us. Whether they are monsters of lust, greed, jealousy, insecurity, or passive. We all have monsters within that we battle to overcome every day."

Dustin ponders his own monsters.

"Some of us have two, or more," Dustin says. "My monsters are jealousy and insecurity. One kept me from going after things that I wanted, things that normally were out of my reach. The Lord bestowed VoLt on me which gave me confidence to beat that monster," Dustin says. "The other nearly killed me."

"Maybe the Lord delivered VoLt to you when you were finally ready. Maybe those insecurities helped keep you on the path that you find yourself on today. False aspirations can often lead to failure. As far as jealousy, well, that's just the Devil's favorite tool."

Dustin knows that the pastor is just trying to cheer him up, but nonetheless, he still struggles with his decisions of late. He pauses as the repercussions of his jealousy start to flood his mind.

"I know a lot of this could have been avoided if I had only cleansed Hank that night at the bar when he and the other Gold Knights were attacked by the group of French men. I just couldn't bring myself to aid him. I intentionally let God down."

He pauses as his heart races and his stomach turns.

"It's no wonder that God took VoLt away from me. I don't deserve it…I failed."

"Dustin, we are all human. We all make mistakes. I don't believe God is punishing you. I think maybe He's trying to get your attention. Maybe to help you refocus."

Pastor Phillips pauses before saying something that he knows may not sit well with Dustin.

"Perhaps there is another test for you on the horizon."

Dustin turns and looks at the pastor with an agitated look, not necessarily directed at Pastor Phillips, just a look of complete aggravation.

Dustin responds. "That's all I need. Another test."

He lightly rolls his eyes as he pulls himself out of the chair across from the pastor's desk and approaches the door. As he reaches for the door knob, the pastor speaks.

"Dustin?"

"Yes?"

"I don't know the path that lies before you. All I can tell you is that you will be in my prayers each and every day as you go on this journey."

Choked up, Dustin didn't respond. He just shakes his head in agreement and steps out.

Moments later, he stands in front of his dresser, staring at it. Taking a deep breath, he approaches the dresser.

Pulling the furniture piece back, he opens the hidden door and unhooks a small gunny sack hanging inside. He empties the contents on his bed and stares at the two old silver metal bracelets.

The bracelets of Evilution rest on his bed.

Dustin's heart races, as it causes a slight shiver in him at the thought of using the hardware of such evil. A feeling of desperation comes over him. He is unable to muster the ability to pray.

His mind is flooded with reasoning and objections on the use of the bracelets.

"I gotta prove to God I want his blessing back. I know I took it for granted."

There's an urge inside him to pray, but he feels so detached from God that he can't bring himself to do it. He looks at the bracelets as his last ditch effort to help Cameron and Jayden while in the meantime, perhaps prove himself to God.

"I don't think I have a choice," he says softly to himself.

Moments later, Dustin sits on his bed, his black cloak encompassing him. He breathes nervously over his impending action. He looks at the address again written on a piece of paper, resting on his night stand. It's Jayden's possible location. He glances over at the clock. 9:47 p.m.

The words that Tim Warner wrote on the newspaper clippings from nearly seventy years ago runs through his mind.

"Make wrong things right."

That had become his mission statement. Trying to right the wrongs that he could under his watch as VoLt. But guilt now consumes him as he seemingly allowed Jayden to fall into danger when Cameron tried desperately to get his attention.

Standing up and walking over, he pops open the hidden secret door as a rush of cold air blew in from the black tunnel. Turning around to face his bed, Dustin reaches down and grabs the bracelets of Evilution and places them on each of his wrist. He holds his breath as the feels the transformation quickly take place over his body. His body contorts and flexes more violently as it did in the past. The rapid feeling of heat flows through his body as his face, hands, feet and back begin to ache as the new form takes place. Finally, feeling the fury burst of his mane, he turns to look at his reflection in the mirror.

"Whew…," he said. "Am I glad to see you."

CHAPTER 50

Dustin, in his altered state, arrives at a dilapidated, seemingly vacant building on the northern part of the city. He can hear commotion of some kind coming from the second floor. Snarling, he cautiously enters the structure through the front doors. The stench of mold, mildew, and rot stings his nose. As he approaches the stairways, shouts echo through the building. Dustin strains to listen.

"How did that pathetic puke get in here?"

Dustin recognizes the voice as Pug's. He quickly advances up the stairs as the yelling continues.

"So, is this what you want?" Pug violently asks, as it echoes throughout the building.

"Please, don't hurt her!" a voice cries out.

Dustin instantly recognizes the other voice, Cameron's. Knowing the situation has quickly turned dangerous, Dustin charges the doors, busting through them like a wild bull. The doors break apart into pieces which causes the current tenants of the dark, musty apartment to take cover and scatter like cockroaches.

Locating Cameron, in the clutch of a couple of the groups' thugs, he discovers that he has everyone's attention. Punk rock music fills the room. Scanning the room, dimly lit by a couple of red bulb lamps, the hairy beast locates the ring leader, Pug.

Pug proceeds to yell profanity at the creature that has crashed their establishment. The beastly Dustin turns his attention to Pug who holds Jayden by the neck with his left hand, while welding a knife in the right.

"Let them go now!" Dustin yells.

The two bullies that held Cameron quickly follows the beastly orders while Pug desperately tries to level the playing field.

"That's it, she's toast!"

He pulls back his right arm in attempt to gain momentum to stab her.

"No!" Dustin roars as he prepares to lunge at Pug.

Instead, Pug has his arm instantly pinned against the wall from seemingly nowhere. Pug looks over only to find Cameron digging his elbow into his chest and a with a death grip on his wrist. Cameron then digs his thumbs into Pug's wrist, forcing him to release the grip on the knife. Jayden takes the opportunity to grab his left wrist and bite with all her might.

Pug screams in pain as he releases Jayden.

Cameron quickly grabs Pug by the throat and yells, "It's over!"

Pug's eyes widen in seemingly utter disbelief at being manhandled by someone whom he pegged as weak. Shaking his head in a motion of showing surrender, he seems to accept his defeat.

Cameron releases Pug by slamming him against the wall.

"That's right, Pug! It's over! I've got the video tape from the pawn shop!" Jayden yells.

Without looking at Jayden, Cameron grabs her hand and turns toward the door.

Pug, instantly fueled with rage, pulls out a gun from the back of his waist. The beastly Dustin roars and charges at Pug, which causes Cameron to turn around. Just as he does, Pug is able to pull the trigger and shoot, hitting Cameron in the upper right shoulder. Pug barely has the shot off before the hairy creature has him pinned against the wall with a violent thud.

Then the beastly Dustin looks at Cameron as he lies on the ground. Jayden screams in terror.

Instantaneously, Dustin is filled with rage. He pulls Pug from the wall only to slam him back again with such force that he creates a deep impression of Pug's head and torso. Pug gasps for air as the creature pulls him back out of the wall only to fling him across the floor. Pug slides across the floor, picking up dirt and trash until he hits the other wall. The beast leaps over to Pug, lifting him up with his left arm, and proceeds to deliver right-handed punches to Pug's face.

"Time to rid the world of your presence!" he growls between punches.

Inside, Dustin is shocked to hear himself utter the words of certain demise.

Suddenly he hears a voice that causes him to stop the beating.

"VoLt, we need you!"

The creature stops the pummeling and turns his attention around only to see Jayden cradling Cameron in her arms. Dustin is shocked by his lack of control. Breathing heavily and suddenly feeling terrified for everyone in the room, he rushes to Cameron's aid.

Cameron is gasping for air as blood trickles from his mouth, Jayden looks at their beastly hero with desperation.

"What do we do?"

Dustin bends down and picks Cameron up with relative ease. He doesn't say anything as he glances around the room and finds Pug lying motionless on the ground. Glancing at Jayden, he nods his head toward the door. She shakes her head yes as they leave the filthy scene.

Moments later, the threesome is running down the street trying to find aid for Cameron. The closest hospital is at least two miles away and the creature doesn't believe Jayden is up for the run. He stops and looks firmly at Jayden.

"Listen to me. We're losing time. Go find his mom. He'll be at London General," he says in direct short sentences.

"But—"

"No buts! Just do it!"

Jayden nods in agreement. He knows he gave her an unwanted task. Being left behind to retrieve Cameron's mom, whom she's never met. Dustin only imagines that this isn't the first encounter Jayden envisioned for finally meeting Cameron's mother.

"Hurry!" he orders as he takes off in a dead sprint for the hospital.

The creature pants heavily as the hospital comes into view. Practically foaming at the mouth he looks for someone to aid them. To his surprise, Cameron speaks.

"You showed up."

The beast looks down at the groggy face addressing him.

"A little late," he growls between pants.

"But you showed up," Cameron responds as he looks up from the creature's cradling arms.

"Save you breath," the beastly Dustin requests.

He looks around and spots a nurse standing along the west wall, sneaking in a cigarette break. The strong straight line of smoke from her mouth indicates an already stressful evening. Dustin knows he's about to make things more intense.

The nurse stands with her back against the wall, her head tilting back resting on her brunette hair bun when she hears heavy breathing approach her. She slowly tilts her head down and gasps as she sees a monstrous creature approach her.

She curses in fear as the beast closes in.

"He needs your help," he says in the calmest voice he can muster.

"What happened to him?" the nurse asks in a terrified manner.

"He's been shot."

"Uh, let me get a stretcher or something," she says as she immediately drops the cigarette and runs inside. Dustin focuses on the fallen cigarette as he watches the red glow fade away. He glances up to see the nurse and a confused orderly push a stretcher to his location. The orderly's wide eyes are his only form of communication as he glances wildly back and forth between the nurse, the beast, and Cameron.

"Place him here," she nurse states the obvious plan.

The creature gingerly lays him down and directs his attention back to the nurse.

"His mother is on the way."

"VoLt. You're VoLt," the orderly says as he finally finds his voice.

The creature just stares back without saying a word.

He reaches down and grabs Cameron's hand and says, "It's going to be all right."

Cameron looks with bewilderment at his would-be hero. The seemingly skeptic look from Cameron indicates that something about this creature's appearance seems different.

Dustin lightly squeezes Cameron's hand. He nods to both of the hospital employees and disappears into the darkness.

CHAPTER 51

Anger continues to run through Dustin's veins as he finds himself back at Pug's residence. In his mind, he had some unfinished business to tend to. The apartment's door is shut as punk rock music still plays. Pushing the doors open violently, he catches a couple of the residents off guard as they try to tend to Pug.

Obscenities flow from their mouths in his direction and he continues to approach the ring leader. A dazed Pug frantically calls on a couple of his cronies to stop him. The beast easily and violently punches and throws the punks around. Suddenly, somewhere, he can hear someone chuckling. He calmly looks around but he can't find the source of the laughter.

He continues toward Pug. Reaching down, he lifts him up as Pug begins to beg for mercy.

"What do you want from me?" he slurs through bloody lips.

Lifting him up and looking at him square in the eyes, he looks for the red glow of evil. To his surprise, the faint glow of evil fades away. Dustin raises his hands up to Pug's face.

"Repent!" he commands.

Nothing happened. The beast growls and roars the command again, "Repent!"

Pug squints at the sure volume of the beast's roar.

"Repent? Okay, Okay, I repent! I won't do it again!" Pug pleads.

Annoyed and alarmed with his inability to cleanse the punk, he feels the anger start to take over.

The creature simply drops Pug as the punk falls to the ground weeping in pain and fear.

Dustin growls and grinds his teeth as he desperately fights internally to contain the rage running out of control in him. His hands shake as he fights the desire to end Pug. Fearful of his own mindset, he turns and bolts for the door.

Dustin quickly runs up the stairway to the rooftop. Bursting through the rooftop's door, he looks over the city. Heart racing with fear, he leaps onto an adjacent building and then on down to the streets where he runs as fast as he can to get home.

Panic races through his veins. Astonished and overwhelmed by this new power, along with his immediate concern to get back to Berthel Church unseen, causes a throbbing pain in his temples. He manages to reach the Underground veins via a manhole cover on a dark street.

This is fun!

The low growling voice that matched the laughter at Pug's hangout catches Dustin off guard as he stops instantly to turn around to see who is following him. To his shock, no one is there. He stands motionless, straining his hearing to hear any movements from the individual who said those creepy haunting words. All he could hear is the steady dripping of water and a subway train way off in the distance.

"Who's there?" Dustin growls back in the same tone. Only his echo answers back.

Dustin realizes that he's standing in attack mode. At that moment, he looks down at the metal bracelets that were strapped around his wrists, his eyes widening at the realization of the location of the voice.

That's right, here I am.

Dustin takes off in a dead sprint down the subway tunnel while the ghostly voice laughs inside Dustin's head.

Finally, Dustin reaches the hidden corridor that leads to his room. He climbs the steep tunnel to the hidden door behind his dresser. With relative ease, he pushes back the dresser and entered his quarters.

I don't like this place!

"Shut up!" Dustin yells as he desperately takes off the bracelets with deliberant force, throwing them on his bed.

Staring at them with bewilderment, quivering and breathing heavily, he asks, "What have I unleashed?"

CHAPTER 52

Weeks later, a red cargo ship pulls in a harbor. Captain Mustavich is standing on the captain's deck overseeing the docking. He receives the message that the ship has docked, to which he turns around and looks at his passenger that is sitting down behind him. The passenger is nursing injuries to his hands that are heavily wrapped in gauze. He appears to still be in severe discomfort as he sits restlessly in his chair. Once the ship is secured, Captain Mustavich turns around and addresses the passenger.

"We have arrived, Professor Zen."

"Very good," Zen responds in a smug tone.

Mustavich responds with a small smirk and he mans the phone and dials a number. A moment passes until the phone call is answered on the other end. The captain proceeds to talk in his native tongue as Zen gingerly stands up, tenderly pulling the shirt out from his scorched chest. His shirt is lightly stained from his own blood.

On the counter next to him, he reaches over and picks up an item that is also wrapped in blood-stained cloth. A gold piece of the object is exposed as Zen deliberately and cautiously avoids coming in contact with it.

VoLt II

Professor Zen learned quickly how to handle the special metal piece with care since it burned whatever part of his body that came in contact with it. Zen has managed to keep the gold medallion's powers a secret from the captain and his shipmates. It is apparent that Zen doesn't understand the powers of it yet. And since this had been an obsession of his for years to acquire the gold V medallion, he wasn't about to lose it now. Along with the victory of finally obtaining the mystical gold medallion, there is the evident agony on his face and disposition that he isn't able to bring the powers of VoLt to himself. The frustration in his face indicates a long journey that somehow, this medallion would eventually unlock the secret powers that have eluded him for so long. But somewhere in the back of his mind had to be the realization that his possession of the V medallion might be his only hope to bring about his other formally owned prize possession, the bracelets of Evilution. One way or another, he is determined to once again possess power that would lead to nations bowing down at his feet.

Zen stands there arrogantly, powering through the evident pain. Preparing himself to get back to work in a new region that was thirsty to heal their god. The aging ruler of the land had been so resourceful in Zen's experiments in the past. The ruler had hoped that Zen would be able to once again bring back his youthfulness that the professor was able to do for himself. Professor Zen acted with confidence that he would be given preferential treatment. The smirk on his face came with an anticipation of an unlimited supply of means and money at his disposal.

As soon as the ship's horn announces its completed docking, a police whistle could be heard coming from the boarding docks. Zen, intrigued by the sudden commotion, went to investigate. Stepping out of the captain's deck, the professor stops in his tracks as he hears the sound of running feet rapidly board the ship and close in on his current location in the captain's office.

The shifting of his eyes indicate a sense of alertness as he re-enters the captain's deck.

"Captain Mustavich, I believe the authorities are boarding your ship." Zen states, looking at the captain with a matter of fact demeanor.

"That is correct, Professor Zen."

The door flew open, and three men point their rifles at Zen.

In a look of disbelief, Zen turns to face Captain Mustavich.

"Time to repay your debt to us," Captain Mustavich said as Zen has handcuffs slapped on his wounded wrists.

CHAPTER 53

The sun shines warmly on the small town of Groves, Montana. The community is nestled in a valley of the Rocky Mountains. Soft white clouds scatter the sky providing shade from the sun for only a moment or two. A yellow jeep pulls up in front of the town's post office, as an attractive light brown haired woman in blue jeans and a black T-shirt hops out with a letter in hand. She recognizes three teenage boys sitting on the bench drinking soda pop and junk food.

"Is this how you spend your Saturday afternoons?" she asked the threesome.

"Uh, yes, Miss Warner," one answers with a smile, showing the chocolate smeared all over his teeth.

The other two quickly wipe their mouths and smile back at Jessie.

"Well, just as long as you're ready for your exam on Monday, I guess that's okay."

She smiles and enters the post office while the boys look at each other and smile and laugh.

"Man, her accent makes me melt," one boy responds.

"Yeah, like the chocolate on your teeth?" the other young man replies.

"Oh…great," he says as he attempts to wipe his mouth. The other two laugh at his instantly flushed face.

Inside, the fifty-year-old postmaster glances up from the counter to see his approaching customer.

"Hello, Jessie," the postmaster greets her with a smile.

"Hello, Walt. How are you today?" she asks.

"Oh, much better now, after seeing your pretty young smile."

Jessie smiles back with a slightly raised eyebrow, as if indicating how surprised he would be if he knew who actually is the younger of the two.

"Thanks, Walt," she replies as she places the envelope on the counter and slides it to him.

"Ah, a letter to London, England," Walt says as he reads the address on the envelope. "Have you been hearing about those creatures running amuck over there?"

Chuckling slightly, Jessie replies, "Yes, I have."

"I swear, I don't know what's coming of this world these days. Just as long as they keep those monsters on their side of the pond," Walt states.

Jessie just smiles with slightly raised eyebrows.

Walt looks at the name on the letter, "An old boyfriend, I assume?"

"No, just a very dear friend."